James Hadley Chase and The Murder Room

>>> This title is part of The Murder Room, our series dedicated to making available out-of-print or hard-to-find titles by classic crime writers.

Crime fiction has always held up a mirror to society. The Victorians were fascinated by sensational murder and the emerging science of detection; now we are obsessed with the forensic detail of violent death. And no other genre has so captivated and enthralled readers.

Vast troves of classic crime writing have for a long time been unavailable to all but the most dedicated frequenters of second-hand bookshops. The advent of digital publishing means that we are now able to bring you the backlists of a huge range of titles by classic and contemporary crime writers, some of which have been out of print for decades.

From the genteel amateur private eyes of the Golden Age and the femmes fatales of pulp fiction, to the morally ambiguous hard-boiled detectives of mid twentieth-century America and their descendants who walk our twenty-first century streets, The Murder Room has it all. >>>

The Murder Room
Where Criminal Minds Meet

themurderroom.com

James Hadley Chase (1906–1985)

Born René Brabazon Raymond in London, the son of a British colonel in the Indian Army, James Hadley Chase was educated at King's School in Rochester, Kent, and left home at the age of 18. He initially worked in book sales until, inspired by the rise of gangster culture during the Depression and by reading James M. Cain's *The Postman Always Rings Twice*, he wrote his first novel, *No Orchids for Miss Blandish*. Despite the American setting of many of his novels, Chase (like Peter Cheyney, another hugely successful British noir writer) never lived there, writing with the aid of maps and a slang dictionary. He had phenomenal success with the novel, which continued unabated throughout his entire career, spanning 45 years and nearly 90 novels. His work was published in dozens of languages and over thirty titles were adapted for film. He served in the RAF during World War II, where he also edited the RAF Journal. In 1956 he moved to France with his wife and son; they later moved to Switzerland, where Chase lived until his death in 1985.

By James Hadley Chase
(published in The Murder Room)

Try This One For Size

James Hadley Chase

An Orion book

Copyright © Hervey Raymond 1980

The right of James Hadley Chase to be identified as the author of this
work has been asserted in accordance with the Copyright, Designs and
Patents Act 1988.

This edition published by
The Orion Publishing Group Ltd
Orion House
5 Upper St Martin's Lane
London WC2H 9EA

An Hachette UK company
A CIP catalogue record for this book is available from the British Library

ISBN 978 1 4719 0404 2

www.orionbooks.co.uk

This one is for John Skalicky

Claude Kendrick, owner of the Kendrick Gallery, back from his August vacation, sat at his desk making plans for another prosperous season.

The heat and the humidity that turned Paradise City, the billionaires' playground, into a dead city was now in the past. September had arrived, and the city was coming alive with the rich, the jet-set and the tourists.

Recognised as a character in the city, Kendrick was a tall, enormously fat queer who resembled a dolphin without, it had been said, the amiable expression of a dolphin. There were times when he resembled a man-eating shark.

Although immaculately dressed at all times, Kendrick, bald as an egg, wore an ill-fitting orange-coloured wig and pale pink lipstick. When he met a lady client on the street, he would raise his wig as if it were a hat. In spite of his enormous bulk and his eccentricities, he was considered in the art world as an expert in antiques, jewellery and modern paintings. His Gallery was known and patronised by the world's collectors. What was not known was that Kendrick was one of the most important and active fences in the United States, and was in constant touch with all the expert art thieves where art treasures were to be found.

Many of Kendrick's clients had their own private museums for their eyes only. It was with these clients that Kendrick

1

did most of his lucrative business. A client would see some art treasure in some museum or in some friend's house and would covet it with that lust only fanatical collectors have. Eventually, unable to control the gnawing urge to possess this particular treasure, he would come to Kendrick and drop a hint: if the so-and-so museum or Mr So-and-so would sell this particular treasure, money would be no object. Knowing the treasure was not for sale at any price, Kendrick would discuss a price, then say he would see what he could arrange. The collector, knowing from past dealings with Kendrick that the affair would work out to his satisfaction, would return to his secret museum and wait. Kendrick would alert one of his many art thieves, discuss terms and also wait. Eventually the art treasure would mysteriously disappear from the so-and-so museum or from Mr So-and-so's collection and arrive at the collector's secret museum. A large sum of money would arrive in Kendrick's Swiss bank in Zurich.

Having spent the month of August on his yacht, sailing the Caribbean sea, in the amusing company of male ballet dancers, Kendrick, refreshed, heavily sun-tanned, took pleasure to be, once again, seated at his desk, turning his expertise and his crooked mind to making money.

Louis de Marney, Kendrick's head salesman, slid into the vast room with its picture window and its antiques in which Kendrick worked.

Louis was thin and could be any age from twenty-five to forty. His long thick hair was the colour of sable. His lean face, close-set eyes and pinched mouth gave him the appearance of a suspicious rat.

"Surprise!" he exclaimed in his high-pitched voice. "You'll never guess! Ed Haddon!"

Kendrick stiffened.

"Here?"

"Waiting!"

Kendrick laid down his gold pencil. His fat face moved into his shark-like smile.

Ed Haddon was the King of art thieves: a brilliant operator who appeared to live the immaculate life of a retired business man, paying his taxes, moving to his various apartments in Fort Lauderdale, the South of France, Paris and London.

Although he had been operating for some twenty years, organising some of the biggest art steals, he had so covered his tracks that the police of the world had no suspicions of his nefarious deals. He was the master-mind who planned, organised and directed a group of experts who did his bidding. It was seldom that he worked with Kendrick, but when he did, the profit for Kendrick was always substantial.

"Hurry, stupid," Kendrick said, lumbering to his feet. "Send him in."

Louis fluttered away, and Kendrick was at the door to greet Haddon, his smile oily, his hand thrust out.

"Ed, darling! What a *lovely* surprise! Come in, come in! You are looking splendid, but then when don't you?"

Ed Haddon stood in the doorway and regarded Kendrick, then he took and shook the offered hand.

"You don't look so lousy yourself except for that god-awful wig," he said, moving into the room.

"It's my trade-mark, Ed, dear boy," Kendrick tittered. "No one would recognise me without it." Still holding Haddon's hand, he led him to a big comfortable chair. "Sit down. Perhaps a glass of champagne?"

Haddon could have been mistaken for a Congressman or even a Secretary of State. His appearance was impressive: tall, heavily built, with thick iron-grey hair, a florid, handsome face, steel-grey eyes and a benign smile which would have earned him a mass of votes had he considered running for Congress. Behind this facade was a razor-sharp brain and a ruthless and cunning mind.

"Scotch on the rocks," he said, taking out a cigar case and selecting a cigar. "Want one of these? Havana."

"Not this early," Claude said, pouring the drink. "I am really delighted to see you after all this time. It's been too long, Ed."

Haddon was looking around the vast room. His eyes examined the various pictures on the silk-covered walls.

"That's nice," he said, pointing to a picture above Kendrick's desk. "Nice brush work. Monet, huh? A fake, of course."

Claude brought the drink and set it on a small antique table by Haddon's side.

3

"Only you and I know that, Ed," he said. "I have an old trout, with too much money, nibbling."

Haddon laughed.

"*After* Monet, huh? Just to cover yourself."

"Of course, dear boy." Claude made himself a dry martini, then went behind his desk and sat down. "It's not often you come to our fair city, Ed."

"Not staying long." Haddon crossed one leg over the other. "How's business, Claude?"

"A little slow. It's the beginning of the season. The antiques will be moving soon. The rich will be back next week."

"I mean . . . business," Haddon said, his steel-grey eyes probing.

"Ah!" Claude shook his head. "Nothing right now. As a matter of fact I could handle something if it came my way."

Haddon lit his cigar and puffed smoke for a long moment.

"I've been trying to decide: whether you or Abe Salisman."

Claude flinched. The name Abe Salisman was always like a drop of acid on his tongue for Salisman was without doubt the biggest fence operating in New York. Many a time he had beaten Kendrick to a big deal. The two men hated each other as a mongoose hates a snake.

"Come now, chéri," he said. "You don't want to deal with a cheap shyster like Abe. You know you can get a better price from me. Have I ever cheated you?"

"You've never had the chance, nor has Abe. This is a matter of big, fast cash. It'll run to six million." Haddon puffed smoke. "I want three."

"Six million isn't impossible," Claude said slowly, his shark-like mind active. "Depends on the goods, of course. There is a lot of money around for something special, Ed."

"There's not all that money right now in New York. That's why I'm giving you the first offer."

Claude put on his dolphin smile.

"Appreciated, dear boy. Tell me."

"The Hermitage exhibition."

"Ah!" The look of greed faded from Kendrick's eyes. "Very nice. I have the catalogue." He opened a desk drawer and produced a thick, glossy brochure. "Yes, very nice. Beautiful items. A gesture of detente. The Russian government lending some of its finest exhibits for the citizens of the United States of America to admire." He flicked through the pages of coloured illustrations. "Magnificent. Thousands taking advantage of this splendid co-operation between two of the most powerful countries." He looked up and eyed Haddon who was smiling. "Yes, but strictly not for you and strictly not for Abe and strictly not for me." He sighed and laid down the catalogue.

"Have you finished shooting off with your mouth?" Haddon asked.

Claude took off his wig, stared at it, then slapped it crookedly back on his head.

"Just thoughts, dear Ed. I often think aloud."

"Look at page fifty-four," Haddon said.

Claude licked his fat thumb and turned the pages of the catalogue.

"Yes. Very nice. What does it say? Icon, date unknown, thought to be the earliest icon in existence. Known to be Catherine the Great's most treasured possession." He regarded the illustration. "Made of wood, painted, showing some unknown Russian saint. Excellent state of preservation. Size 8 by 10 inches. Not everyone's choice. The mob would pass it by. Very interesting as a collector's piece."

"In the open market, it would be worth twenty million dollars," Haddon said quietly.

"I'll accept that, but obviously the Russians wouldn't sell, dear boy."

Haddon leaned forward, his steel-grey eyes like the points of ice picks.

"Could you sell it, Claude?"

Kendrick found that in spite of the air-conditioning, he was sweating slightly. He took a silk handkerchief from his pocket and wiped his face.

"It is possible to sell anything, but this icon could cause trouble."

"Never mind the trouble. It's yours for three million," Haddon said.

5

Kendrick finished his martini. He felt in need of another.

"Let me refresh your drink, Ed. This needs a little thought."

He plodded over to the liquor cabinet and made two more drinks, his mind very active.

"I haven't much time," Haddon said accepting the drink. "The exhibition closes in two weeks. It's either to be you or Abe."

Claude returned to his desk and sat down.

"Let's look closely at this, Ed," he said. "I visited the Fine Arts Museum when I was in Washington a year ago. It seemed to me then that their security precautions were impressive. I understand from what I've read that the security precautions for this exhibition have been tightened and the chances of a steal there are nil."

Haddon nodded.

"Oh, sure. I've gone into all that. Not only have the museum guards been increased, but the Feds and the CIA, and plain clothes cops are swarming all over. Not only that but the Russians have supplied five of their own cops to add to the merry crowd. All visitors are checked. No man or woman is allowed to take in a bag or a handbag. All visitors go through the electronic screen. Yeah, I admit they have done an impressive job."

Claude lifted his fat shoulders.

"So . . ."

"Yeah. I like handling impossible steals, Claude. I have never failed to get what I want, and I'm telling you if you can sell the icon and pay me three million bucks into my Swiss account, the icon is yours."

Claude thought back on the various big steals Haddon had organised. He remembered the five-foot-high Ming vase that disappeared from the British Museum. That had been a masterpiece of organisation, but he hesitated. This was something different: the political angle would be dangerous.

"Let us suppose you get the icon, Ed," he said cautiously. "I don't have to tell you this will cause an international incident or let us say an explosion. The heat will be very fierce."

"That's your funeral, Claude. Once I give you the icon,

6

you cope with the heat, but if you don't want to handle it, say so and I'll talk to Abe."

Kendrick hesitated, then the thought of a three-million-dollar profit overcame his caution.

"Give me three days, Ed. I must talk to a client or two."

"Fair enough. I'm at the Spanish Bay hotel. Let me know not later than Friday night. If you can find the right client, you'll get the icon the following Tuesday."

Kendrick wiped the sweat off his face.

"Just to reassure me, dear Ed, tell me how you are going to get it."

Haddon got to his feet.

"Later. You get the client first, then we'll have a talk about ways and means." He stared long at Kendrick. "I'll get it. You don't have to worry about that. See you," and he left.

Kendrick sat thinking, then he opened one of the desk drawers and took out a leather-bound book in which he kept the names and addresses of his richest clients, all of them with secret museums.

Louis de Marney came fluttering in.

"What did he want, darling?" he asked. "Business?"

Kendrick waved him away.

"Don't bother me," he said. "Don't let anyone bother me. I have to think."

Knowing the signs, Louis left silently, closing the door. Big money was in the pipe-line, and as Louis had a fifteen per cent share in Kendrick's illegal operations, he was content to wait until his assistance was required.

It took Kendrick well over an hour to decide which of his clients he should approach. He needed someone interested in Russian art and who could raise six million dollars at short notice. Discarding name after name for one reason or another, principally because of their lack of interest in Russian art, he finally turned to the R's.

Herman Radnitz!

Of course! He should have thought of him at once.

Herman Radnitz had once been described by a journalist working for *Le Figaro* as follows:

"Radnitz is Mr Big Business. Suppose you want a dam

built in Hong Kong. Suppose you want to launch a car-ferry service between England and Denmark. Suppose you want to install electrical equipment in China. Before you even begin to make plans, you consult Radnitz who would fix the financial end. Radnitz is in practically everything: ships, oil, building construction, aircraft, and he has strong connections with the Soviet government, and he is on first name terms with the President of the United States of America. He's probably the richest man, outside Saudi Arabia, in the world."

Yes, Radnitz, Kendrick thought, but this would have to be handled very carefully.

After more thought, he put through a call to the Belvedere hotel where he knew Radnitz was staying.

After talking to Gustav Holtz, Radnitz's secretary, Kendrick was granted an interview at 10:00 the following morning.

During the month of August, crime in Paradise City had been practically non-est. Apart from a few stolen cars and old ladies reporting the loss of their dogs, the police in this humid, sweaty city had little to do.

Chief of Police Fred Terrell was on vacation. Sergeant Joe Beigler, left in charge of the Cop house, spent his time in Terrell's office, drinking coffee and chain-smoking. Being an active man, he would have liked nothing better than a big jewel robbery or some such thing, but the thieves and the con-men didn't arrive until the rich and the jet-set returned towards the middle of September.

In the Detectives' room, Detective 1st Grade Tom Lepski, tall dark and lean, had his feet on his desk while reading the comics. At another desk, Detective 2nd Grade Max Jacoby, four years younger than Lepski, dark and powerfully built, hammered out a stolen-car report on his ancient typewriter.

The activity in the Detectives' room, compared to six weeks ago, was as animated as the city's morgue.

Jacoby yanked the paper and carbons from his typewriter and sat back.

"That's that," he said. "What else is there to do?"

"Nothing." Lepski yawned. "Why don't you go home?

8

No point in both of us sitting around."

"I'm doing the shift until 22.00, worse luck. You go home."

Lepski gave a sly grin.

"Oh, no. I'm not that crazy in the head. If I go home now, Carroll will insist I cut the lawn, and who wants to cut a goddamn lawn in this heat?"

Jacoby nodded agreement.

"You have a point. Phew! This heat kills me. We should have air-conditioning here."

"Talk to the Chief. You could persuade him. Anyway, it'll be cooler in another few days."

"How about your vacation, Tom? You're off next week, aren't you? Where are you going?"

Lepski released a laugh that would have frightened a hyena.

"Me? I'm going nowhere. I'm staying home. I'm going to sit in the garden and read a book."

"A book?" Jacoby gaped. "I didn't know you read books."

"I don't, but what the hell? It'll make a change. I want to find out if I'm missing anything. From the look of the pictures on some of the books, I just could."

Jacoby thought for a long moment, frowning.

"How about Carroll?" he asked finally.

Lepski looked shifty.

"There'll be a little trouble, but I will handle it," he said, unease in his voice. "You know something? Carroll has crazy ideas. Right now, she is reading travel brochures. She wants us to tour California in a coach. Imagine! You know what these travel thieves want to take you all over California? Three weeks for three thousand dollars! Crazy! Anyway who wants to travel with a load of finks in a lousy coach? Not me!"

Jacoby considered this.

"Well, it's a way of seeing the country. I wouldn't mind it. Carroll would have a ball. She likes chatting up people."

Lepski released a snort that fluttered the newspaper on his desk.

"Listen, Max, no can do. I'm up to my eyes in back payments. Everytime I walk into my bank the teller stares at me as if I were a heist man. Tonight, I'm going to explain the situation to Carroll. I've got out a balance sheet. Okay, she'll scream the house down, but figures are facts. She'll have to sit on the lawn and read a book like I'm going to do."

Jacoby, who was a close friend both of Lepski and his bossy wife, Carroll, hid a grin.

"Can't see Carroll agreeing to that," he said.

Lepski glared at him.

"If there's no money, there's no vacation. I've still to pay for that hair-dryer she bought. I'm late on the car payments." He drew in a long breath. "Then I'm late on that goddamn TV set she wanted. So . . . no money . . . no vacation."

"I'm sorry, Tom. You and Carroll need a vacation."

"So what? We'll have to do what thousands of finks are doing . . . stay at home." Lepski got to his feet and wandered into the Chief's office where he found Sergeant Beigler dozing behind Terrell's desk.

Beigler, freckled with sandy hair, yawned, rubbed a powerful fleshy hand over his face and grinned at Lepski.

"How I hate this month," he said. "Nothing doing. You're off next week on vacation . . . right?"

"Yeah." Lepski prowled around the office. "As soon as I go, I bet action starts. Listen, Joe, I'm not going away. I'm staying home, so if you want me, for God's sake, call me."

"Not going away? What's Carroll going to say?" Beigler, like Jacoby, knew Carroll.

"No money: no vacation," Lepski said firmly, although he experienced a qualm. Carroll and he often fought although they wouldn't have been parted for the world. Unfortunately for him, Carroll always seemed to win their fights, and of this he was acutely aware. But this time, he kept telling himself, she must accept facts and be reasonable.

"You're a betting man, Tom," Beigler said with a cunning smile. "I'll bet you ten to one you do take a vacation."

Lepski became alert.

"Make that in hundreds and you're on," he said.

Beigler shook his head.

"To win a hundred off me, you'd break a leg, you Shylock."

The telephone bell rang. Charley Tanner, the desk sergeant, was having trouble with a rich old lady who had mislaid her cat.

"Go and help him, Tom," Beigler said wearily. "It'll help pass the time."

At 18:30, Lepski signed off. The air was cooler, and he decided this was the right time to talk to Carroll, and even cut the goddamn lawn. First, he decided, he would do the lawn, then have supper, then explain carefully to Carroll just why a vacation this year was not on.

He arrived at his cosy bungalow with his usual screeching of brakes. If nothing else, Lepski was a show-off, and he liked to impress his neighbours when he returned home. The finks, as he called them, were, as usual, in their gardens. They all gaped as Lepski got out of his car. This was something he liked, and he gave them a condescending wave of his hand, then he paused, and it was his turn to gape.

His lawn looked immaculate. When he had left home in the morning, the grass had been two inches high. Now, it looked like a billiard table: even the edges of the lawn had been trimmed: something he never did.

Carroll?

He pushed his hat to the back of his head. That wasn't possible. Carroll was a dim-wit when handling the power mower. Only once had he persuaded her to have a try, and the result had been a damaged front gate and the loss of one of the rose beds.

Puzzled he walked up the path, opened the front door, and immediately his nose twitched. The smell of cooking that wafted out of the kitchen brought his gastric juices to attention.

Usually, the smell coming from the kitchen to greet him made him wonder if the bungalow was on fire. Although Carroll was an ambitious cook, her efforts invariably ended in disaster. The smell that was now greeting him came as a shock.

Cautiously he entered the small lobby and peered into the

11

living room. Here again, he experienced a shock. On one of the small tables in the centre of the room was a vase filled with long-stemmed roses. Usually, Carroll cut the rather tired-looking roses from the garden, but these, in the vase, were the kind of roses some sucker would give a movie star in the hope of dragging her into his bed.

A sudden chill ran through Lepski. Was this day an anniversary he had forgotten? Lepski was hopeless about anniversaries. Had it not been for Max Jacoby who kept a birthday book and reminded Lepski,—Carroll's birthday would have been forgotten.

What anniversary? Lepski stood gaping at the roses, trying to remember the date of his wedding anniversary. He knew it couldn't be Carroll's birthday. Only five months ago, Jacoby had saved him from disaster. But *what* anniversary?

Carroll was very touchy about any missed anniversary. Lepski thought she was a nut about such dreary affairs. She considered it of vital importance that he should remember her birthday, his birthday, their wedding anniversary, the day he got promoted to First grade, the day they moved into their bungalow. If forgotten, she would make Lepski's life miserable for at least a week.

Lepski braced himself. He would have to play this off the cuff. He wished to God he could remember the date of their wedding anniversary: that was the important one. If he had slipped up on this one, he knew he would be in the dog-house for a month.

Then he heard Carroll, clattering pots and pans in the kitchen, burst into song. Her rendering of *You, Me and Love* set his teeth on edge. Carroll was no singer, but she had lots of lung power.

Dazed, Lepski moved to the kitchen door and stared at his dark, pretty wife, wearing an apron and dancing around the kitchen, beating time to her singing with a wooden spoon.

Jesus! he thought. She's been at my Cutty Sark!

"Hi, baby," he said huskily, "I'm back."

Carroll threw the spoon in the air and descended on him, wrapping her arms around him and giving him the sexiest kiss since their honeymoon.

"Tom, darling! Hmm! Lovely! Again!"

Cutty Sark or not, Lepski reacted. His hands roved down

12

her long slim back and over her buttocks, pulling her hard against him.

Carroll pushed him firmly away.

"Not now: later. Here, make yourself useful," and leaving him, standing dazed, she waltzed to the refrigerator and produced a bottle of champagne. "Open this. Dinner in a moment."

Lepski gaped at the bottle and nearly dropped it.

"But, baby . . ."

"Open it." She returned to the stove and turned two enormous steaks, shifting a mass of frying onions, then stirring the crisping potatoes.

"Sure . . . sure." Lepski wrestled with the wire, then with brute strength, wrenched out the cork which flew across the kitchen. The wine began to bubble out, and Carroll thrust two glasses at him. He filled the glasses, still in a daze.

"To us!" Carroll cried dramatically, taking a glass from him. "The loveliest people on earth!"

"Yeah," Lepski said, and began to wonder if any of his Cutty Sark Scotch was left.

"Come on, let's eat!" Carroll exclaimed and emptied her glass. "Open the wine. It's on the table."

"Sure." Lepski walked flat-footed into their little dining room.

The table had been set, there was a bowl of roses as a centre piece and a bottle of the best Californian red wine waiting his attention.

He began doing sums in his head. The champagne . . . the wine . . . the roses! Jesus! She must have spent all the housekeeping money!

Carroll came in carrying two plates, loaded with the steaks, fried onions and potato chips.

"Enjoy it!" she said, sitting down. "I'll pour the wine."

Hunger overcame Lepski's fears. He hadn't eaten a better steak within memory. He began to wolf.

"Marvellous!" he exclaimed, his mouth full. Then a thought struck him. "A steak like this must have cost a fortune."

"It did," Carroll said, looking smug. "It came from Eddies."

Lepski paused in his eating, feeling a chill run through

him. Eddies was the most expensive steak-house in the city. He had often peered through their windows at the tempting, juicy-looking meat, then seeing the prices, had hurried away in horror.

"Eddies, huh?"

"The best."

"Yeah." He began to eat more slowly. "I see you cut the lawn, honey. Looks nice. I could have done it."

"I got Jack to do it. I didn't want you to have to do it in this heat."

"Jack? The little fink next door? *He* did it?"

"For five dollars he would shoot his father."

"*Five dollars*? You gave that little bastard *five dollars*?"

"He wanted ten but I talked him around."

Lepski closed his eyes.

"Eat up, darling. Don't sit there looking like a street accident." Carroll giggled. "It's all right. I'll let you into a secret."

Lepski eyed her.

"Look, baby, is this some goddamn anniversary I've forgotten? You've been spending money like crazy. You know we haven't any money."

"I know *you* haven't any money, but *I* have."

Lepski's eyes narrowed.

"Since when?"

"Since this morning. You remember Mr Ben Isaacs, my special client when I worked at the American Express?"

"Sure. The old fink who had his hand up your skirt every time he came into the office."

"Lepski! Don't be coarse! Mr Isaacs never did such a thing!"

Lepski leered.

"Maybe, but it was in his mind . . . the same thing."

"Let me tell you, Lepski, Mr Isaacs was a nice, decent old gentleman with a heart of gold."

Lepski pointed like a gun dog.

"You mean he's croaked?"

"He died, and he remembered me in his will. What do you think of that?"

14

Lepski laid down his knife and fork.

"How much?"

"Never mind how much. Wasn't he kind? After all, I was only doing my job and . . ."

"How much?" Lepski bawled in his cop voice.

"Don't shout at me, Lepski." Carroll began to eat again. "Don't let your dinner get cold."

"HOW MUCH?" Lepski bawled.

Carroll sighed, but there was laughter in her eyes.

"If you must know: thirty thousand dollars."

"THIRTY THOUSAND DOLLARS?" Lepski screamed, starting to his feet.

Carroll smiled at him.

"Isn't it wonderful? Do sit down and eat. Try to act civilised."

Lepski sat down, but he had lost his appetite.

Thirty thousand dollars! A goddamn fortune! He thought of all his debts. To think an old fink like Ben Isaacs would leave them all that money!

"You really mean we are worth thirty thousand dollars?" he asked huskily.

"I didn't say that."

Lepski stared.

"Now, hold it. You've just said . . ."

"I know what I said. I told you *I* was now worth thirty thousand dollars. I didn't say anything about *us* being worth thirty thousand dollars," Carroll said firmly.

Lepski gave her his sexy smile.

"The same thing, baby. We're partners . . . remember? We are married. We share and share alike."

"We do nothing of the kind." Carroll finished her steak, then sat back. "Now listen to me," she went on in her bossy voice. "We have been married for five years. Every year we have gone off on some crummy vacation and you've grumbled about the expense. You spent most of our vacation time writing figures and telling me we can't afford lobster or even a coke! I am now going on a *real* vacation, Lepski! I am arranging it all myself. I am going to spend *my* money. If I want champagne for breakfast, I am going to have cham-

15

pagne for breakfast! I am going to Europe. I am going to Paris. I am going to Monte Carlo. I am going to Switzerland to see the mountains. I am staying at the best hotels. I am eating at the best restaurants. I intend to have a vacation of a life time: all paid by dear Mr Ben Isaacs, bless his kind, thoughtful heart!"

Lepski gaped at her.

"Now, wait a minute . . ."

"Quiet! You are invited. You will be my guest. You can either accept or you can stay at home, but *I* am going!"

"But, honey, let's be sensible. We owe money. This will cost a fortune."

"Lepski! *You* owe money! *I* don't! Are you coming with me or aren't you? If you come with me, we fly to Paris next Thursday. If you don't accept my invitation, I fly alone. What's it to be?"

Lepski accepted the inevitable.

"Try and stop me, baby," he said and jumping up, he ran around the table to kiss her.

She hugged him.

"Isn't it wonderful! Oh, Tom, it's going to be something we'll talk about all the rest of our days! I'm going to buy a camera. Imagine how the neighbours will gape when I show them the photos!"

Lepski brightened. There was nothing he liked better than to impress his neighbours.

"Yeah. Paris, huh? Monte Carlo, huh? Switzerland? Jesus, won't I bend Max's ears back tomorrow!"

"I am going to be busy," Carroll said dreamily. "First, I'm going to talk to Miranda. I want her to lay on the trip. She and I worked at the American Express and she knows her stuff. Then I'm going to buy clothes! Imagine! I haven't a decent rag to my back!"

Lepski flinched.

"Now, look, baby, don't get too extravagant. We don't want to over-spend."

"Quiet! And I'll tell you something, Lepski. I am going to buy you some clothes. I'm not travelling with you looking like a bum."

Lepski stiffened.

16

"Are you calling me a bum? What's the matter with the way I look? I don't need a thing! Bum? What do you mean?"

Carroll sighed.

"Just be quiet. You are going away looking like a well-to-do *handsome* husband, and not like a cop."

Lepski cocked an eyebrow.

"Handsome, huh?"

"Handsome, huh?"

"Terribly handsome and sexy, Tom."

Lepski puffed out his chest.

"Yeah. I guess I should dress the part. Handsome and sexy, huh? Okay, baby, let's spend a little money." He paused, then sniffed. "Is something burning?"

Carroll gave a stifled scream.

"My apple pie!"

She sprang up and rushed to the kitchen. Her wail of despair, which Lepski had heard so often, made him grab his napkin to stifle a raucous laugh.

two

Under the shade of the awning, Herman Radnitz sat on the terrace of his penthouse suite at the Belvedere hotel, studying a legal document.

With his hooded eyes, beaky nose, almost lipless mouth, the mottle colour of his skin and his short, fat body, Radnitz resembled a repellent toad. His appearance never bothered him. He had money and power, and it amused him to see how men and women fawned over him, especially women.

This morning, he was putting together a deal that would net him even more money. There were a few legal problems to iron out, but Radnitz was a master at ironing out legal problems.

He glanced up, his hooded eyes showing irritation as Gustav Holtz, his secretary, came silently across the terrace.

Gustav Holtz, some fifty years of age, was tall, thin and balding, with deep-set eyes and a cruel mouth. He was a mathematical genius, a man with no scruples, with eight languages at his finger tips, and with a shrewd political know-how. He was as important to Radnitz as Radnitz's right hand.

"What is it?" Radnitz snapped. "I am busy!"

"Claude Kendrick is here, sir," Holtz said. "Do you want to see him? It was agreed he should come here this morning."

Radnitz laid down the document.

"I will see him." He pointed to the document. "Look at this, Holtz: clause ten. I don't like it. We must do better than this."

Holtz picked up the document, then went into the penthouse suite. A moment later, Kendrick, immaculately dressed in a sky-blue linen suit, his wig carefully combed and on straight, and carrying a briefcase, came across the terrace.

Radnitz eyed him malevolently.

"What do you want? I am busy!"

Kendrick was frightened of Radnitz, but he knew this man had the money he wanted. His fat face creased into an oily smile.

"Busy? When aren't you, Mr Radnitz?" he purred, advancing to the table. "Forgive me for intruding, but I have something that just, just might be of interest to you."

Radnitz shrugged, then waved to a chair.

"What? Sit down!"

Kendrick lowered his bulk on to the chair.

"So kind, Mr Radnitz. It is a great privilege . . ."

"What is it?" Radnitz barked.

Kendrick winced. This dreadful man, he warned himself, was in a bad mood. Kendrick realised his usual soft-soap approach would only irritate Radnitz. He came immediately to the crux of his proposition.

"The Hermitage exhibition in Washington," he said.

A look of interest appeared in Radnitz's hooded eyes.

"What about it?"

"You may not have seen the catalogue. Splendid treasures . . . marvellous . . ."

"I've seen it. What about it?"

Kendrick took from his briefcase the illustrated catalogue of the exhibition. He opened it at page fifty-four, then reverently laid the open catalogue on the table. He pushed the catalogue towards Radnitz.

"This magnificent item."

Radnitz picked up the catalogue and studied the illustrated icon. He read the details, his face expressionless, then he looked at Kendrick.

"So?"

"A remarkable, unique treasure," Kendrick said, smiling

his dolphin smile. "Possibly the first icon . . ."

"I can read," Radnitz snapped. "What's this to me?"

"I understand, sir, that, on the open market, this icon is worth at least twenty million dollars."

Radnitz laid down the catalogue, his eyes cloudy.

"That is possible, but this icon is not for sale. It is the property of the Soviet Union."

"Of course, Mr Radnitz, but things happen. Let us suppose that this icon comes on the market. Would you be interested in buying it for say, eight million dollars?"

Radnitz sat for a long moment, staring at Kendrick who smiled hopefully at him.

"Are you serious?" Radnitz asked, a rasp in his voice.

"Yes, sir . . . very serious," Kendrick returned, his smile drooping a little.

Radnitz got to his feet and walked over to a bank of flowers bordering the terrace. He stood with his back to Kendrick and stared down at the beach and the sea, his mind busy.

Watching him, Kendrick felt his heart flutter.

'The fish nibbles,' he thought.

Radnitz remained still for some five minutes. The long wait made Kendrick mop his face, but he hitched on his smile when Radnitz returned to the table and sat down.

"The icon is not coming on the open market," Radnitz said.

"No, but for a private collector who is interested in acquiring this marvellous treasure, an arrangement could be made."

"What arrangement?"

"I have been assured that if I can find a buyer, the icon will be delivered. I wouldn't be here, sir, unless I was satisfied this can be arranged."

"When?"

Kendrick drew in a long, soft breath. The fish was hooked!

"Some time next week, provided eight million dollars are deposited in a Swiss bank account."

Radnitz took a cigar from a box on the table and went through the ritual of lighting the cigar.

"I hope for your sake, Kendrick," he said, a vicious glare

21

in his eyes, "you mean what you are saying."

"You can rely on me, sir," Kendrick began to sweat again.

"I haven't forgotten the Russian stamps you promised to deliver, and what happened."

Kendrick sighed.

"That was unfortunate. I can't be blamed for what did happen.*"

"I will give you that," Radnitz said grudgingly. "All right, I will buy the icon from you for six million dollars, and no more. You can take it or leave it."

This was better than Kendrick had hoped. It would mean he would make a three-million-dollar profit.

"Sir, I must remind you an operation like this has to be financed," he said, his oily smile in evidence. "I suggest six million and expenses."

"Don't try to haggle with me!" Radnitz snarled. "Here is my offer. The icon is to be delivered to me at my villa in Zurich. On delivery, I will arrange payment of six million dollars to be credited to a bank you name. That is my final offer."

Kendrick stiffened as if touched by a red hot iron.

"Zurich?" His voice shot up. "That isn't possible, sir. How can I get such a treasure out of America to Zurich? You will realise that once the icon is missing..."

Radnitz cut him short with a wave of his hand.

"I'm not interested in problems. All I am interested in is to receive the icon in Zurich. If you are not capable of getting the icon to Zurich, say so. I am busy."

Kendrick faltered. This was something he had to talk over with Haddon.

"It will be very difficult," he muttered.

"It is never easy to earn six million dollars," Radnitz snapped, tipping the ash off his cigar. "Go away and consider my offer. If my secretary has not heard from you in three days to say you can arrange this, then never bother me in the future with other offers." He leaned forward, his eyes glaring. "Do you understand?"

★ See: *You're Dead Without Money*.

Sweat was now running down Kendrick's face. He got unsteadily to his feet.

"Yes, Mr Radnitz. I will do the best I can."

Radnitz dismissed him with a wave of his hand.

Kendrick drove immediately to the Spanish Bay hotel where he found Ed Haddon finishing a late breakfast. As Kendrick plodded towards him, Haddon signalled to a waiter to bring more coffee.

Kendrick sat down heavily at the table. His greedy little eyes surveyed the remains of crisp bacon on a serving dish.

"Coffee?" Haddon asked.

"That would be nice."

The two men looked at each other, then Kendrick gave a slight nod of his head.

Neither of the men said anything until coffee had been served and the waiter had gone away, then Haddon said, "It's on?"

"Let us say I have found a buyer," Kendrick said. "It is now up to you."

"How much?"

"You will be paid three million."

Haddon smiled.

"Three million and expenses, of course."

"Three million, dear Ed: no expenses," Kendrick said firmly.

"The setting up of the operation will cost forty thousand dollars in bribe money, Claude. I'm not paying that. That's your end of the deal."

"No. It's your end of the deal, Ed."

"Okay. I'll talk to Abe. It could take time, but he'll come up with a buyer."

Kendrick smiled his shark's smile.

"I would be prepared to halve the expenses. No more."

"You can rely on your buyer?"

"Of course."

Haddon shrugged.

"Twenty in cash?"

"If you insist."

"We have a deal. The operation is in the pipe-line, but there's one thing I will want from you. I will need a replica of the icon: nothing elaborate: just something that will deceive the eye for a couple of hours."

"You are planning a substitution?"

"Never mind. I have it all worked out. Can you get me a replica within three days?"

Kendrick nodded.

"Louis can do it." He stared thoughtfully at Haddon. "You seem very confident. I only hope this comes off. I could be in serious trouble if you fail. My client is a dangerous man: a dreadful man. I have promised him the icon sometime next week."

"You will have it Tuesday evening," Haddon said quietly.

"You really mean this in spite of the difficulties?"

"You will have it Tuesday evening," Haddon repeated.

Kendrick sighed, thinking this was only the beginning. He fully realised what an explosion the stealing of the icon would cause. Every exit from the States would be slammed shut. The FBI and the CIA, the police, the customs people would be alerted. If only he could have taken the icon to Radnitz at his hotel and have been shot of it! But Zurich!

He got heavily to his feet, wishing now he hadn't approached Radnitz.

"I'll get Louis to bring you the replica and twenty thousand in cash." He paused, standing over Haddon. "Ed, I trust you. There is going to be a dreadful fuss once it is missed. I really can't see how you can possibly get it, but if you say so, I must hope you can."

Haddon smiled.

"You are getting too fat, Claude."

"I know. Louis is always on at me about my weight." Kendrick took off his wig, stared at it, then slapped it back crookedly.

Three million dollars!

Bracing himself, he waved, and plodded across the terrace to where he had parked his car.

Louis de Marney was completing a nice sale of a pair of George IV candlesticks when Kendrick entered the gallery. One look at Kendrick's crooked wig alerted Louis that something was wrong. Kendrick didn't even pause to gush over the elderly client who was writing a cheque. He went straight to his office, closed the door, then went to the small refrigerator, cunningly disguised as an antique commode. When under stress, Kendrick had need of food. He selected a wing of chicken, wrapped it in a crisp lettuce leaf then sat down at his desk.

He was just finishing the little snack when Louis bounced in.

"What's wrong?" he demanded, coming to the desk. "You are eating again!"

"Don't bully me, chéri," Kendrick said. "I have a job for you."

Louis eyed him suspiciously as Kendrick took the Hermitage catalogue from his briefcase and turned to page fifty-four.

"I need a replica of this, dear boy. Nothing special. I'm sure your talent will run something up looking like this."

Louis stared at the icon, then took a quick step back.

"Don't tell me that dreadful Haddon is planning to steal this?" he demanded, his voice shrill.

"I have a buyer for it," Kendrick said softly. "Now, don't get alarmed, chéri. Just make a replica."

"Have you gone out of your mind?" Louis shrilled. "Don't you realize all these things belong to the Soviet Union? Haddon must have gone mad! No, I want nothing to do with it! You mustn't have anything to do with it! Baby, think! Our lives could be utterly ruined!"

Kendrick sighed.

"Perhaps I was a little hasty, but Ed is absolutely certain he can get it. Ed has never let us down, has he?"

"I don't care! This is something we don't touch!" Louis said, glaring at Kendrick. "I will not have anything to do with it! Suppose this dreadful Haddon does get the icon? What are you going to do with it? You must know that it is quite, quite unsaleable! Every beastly cop in the world will be watching for it. The Government will flip their horrid lids! The Russians will be utterly vicious."

"Radnitz wants it," Kendrick said.

Louis reared back.

"That ghastly creature! Have you been mad enough to talk to him?"

"I am committed, chéri."

"Then it's your funeral! I repeat I will have absolutely nothing to do with it!"

Kendrick forced an oily smile.

"Your share of the take, chéri, will be four hundred and fifty thousand dollars."

"I will have nothing to do . . ." Louis paused, his little eyes suddenly calculating. "How much did you say?"

"Yes, dear boy. This is a very big deal. Your share will be four hundred and fifty thousand dollars."

"All I will have to do is to make a replica?"

"No, dear boy, a little more than that," Kendrick said. "That is a lot of money. You must expect to do more than make a replica."

"What else?"

"There is a problem to solve. Ed will deliver the icon to me on Tuesday. Radnitz insists the icon be delivered to him in Zurich."

Louis reacted as if he had been stung by a hornet.

"*Where*?" he screamed.

"Zurich, Switzerland," Kendrick said, "and for heaven's sake, chéri, don't make so much noise."

"Switzerland?" Louis repeated, the dream of owning nearly half a million dollars suddenly fading. "Are you out of your mind? Every exit will be watched! Interpol will be alerted! The heat will be unbearable! Every suspect art dealer will be plagued! *Zurich*? Impossible! Claude, you have been utterly irresponsible to have dealt with that dreadful creature!".

"Nothing is impossible," Kendrick said quietly. "We have until Tuesday. Between then and now, we must think."

Louis looked at him suspiciously.

"You are not expecting *me* to try to smuggle this thing out, are you?"

Kendrick had considered this might be a possibility, but decided Louis hadn't the nerve.

"No, chéri, but there must be a safe way." Kendrick

26

pushed the catalogue towards Louis. "First things first. Make the replica, and think."

Louis hesitated, then thought of the money he had been promised.

"At least, I will do that," he said, "but I'm warning you that this is a mad and dangerous operation."

"Let us both think. It is possible Ed will fail, but we must be ready. It is surprising what ingenuity and thought will produce."

"Tell that to the deaf, dumb and blind," Louis said. He snatched up the catalogue and flounced out.

Feeling in need of another snack, Kendrick plodded to the refrigerator and regarded the various dishes set out in readiness, then selecting a lobster tail, he returned to his desk and sat down to think.

In his usual show-off manner, Lepski arrived home, pounded up the path, threw open the front door and charged into the living-room.

He had had a splendid day telling Beigler and Max Jacoby how Carroll had inherited money, how he had insisted they should spend it on a trip to Europe. He bored the two men to distraction, but this was his big moment, and neither of them could stop him. Finally, Beigler suggested he should go home, and leave them to cope with whatever crime happened, and if there was anything important, he would be called.

"Hi, baby!" Lepski bawled. "I'm back! What's for dinner?"

Carroll was lying on the settee, her shoes off, her eyes closed.

"Must you shout?" she complained. "I'm exhausted."

Lepski gaped at her.

"Have you been jogging or something?"

At this hour, Carroll was usually coping in the kitchen, preparing dinner. To see her lying on the settee, inactive, was a shock to Lepski.

"There are times, Lepski, when I think you are stupid," Carroll said tartly. "I have been arranging our vacation, and

27

let me tell you, I have been at it all day."

"Yeah: tough. What's for dinner?"

Carroll glared.

"Can't you think of anything else except food?"

Lepski leered at her.

"Well, there is another thing, baby, but I'd get the old routine: not now, later. What's for dinner?"

"I don't know. I've been at the American Express all day and I am tired."

Lepski regarded his wife, then recognizing the signs he decided the situation had to be handled with tact and soft soap.

"Poor baby. All day, huh? How's it going? What have you fixed?"

"Miranda has her ideas and I have mine!" Carroll exclaimed. "She couldn't get into her silly head that we want to travel first class. She kept on and on about charter flights."

"What's wrong with charter flights, for God's sake?"

"Lepski! This is a vacation to end all vacations! We are travelling first class!"

"Fine . . . fine. Yeah, you're right, baby." Lepski shifted from one foot to the other. "What's for dinner?"

Carroll sat up, her eyes stormy.

"I don't know! I don't care! If you say that again I will divorce you!"

"Don't know, huh? Okay, let's have a drink." Lepski went to the liquor cabinet. He opened the doors, then started back. "Where's my Cutty Sark?"

"Will you please sit down and listen to what I have arranged?" Carroll said, her voice suddenly on the defensive.

"Where's my Cutty Sark?" Lepski bawled.

"Can't you think of anything but food and drink? For goodness sake, sit down and let me tell you what I have arranged."

Lepski stared at her accusingly.

"You have been around to that drunken old sot, Mehitabel Bessinger, and you've given that old fake my Cutty Sark."

To his surprise, Carroll looked sheepish.

"Now, Tom. I'm sorry about your Scotch. I shouldn't have gone to see her. I have come to the conclusion you are

28

right. She does drink too much."

Lepski gaped at her.

For years now, Carroll had put her faith in this old clair-voyante: a large black woman who foretold the future. Twice she had given Lepski, through Carroll, clues to killers which he had ignored only to find, later, she had been right. Up to now, Carroll had sworn by her. This sudden change startled Lepski.

"What are you saying?" he demanded, sitting down.

"Well, Tom, I thought it might be a good idea to consult her about our trip," Carroll said, looking anywhere but at him.

Lepski made a noise like a fall of gravel.

"So to oil her works, you took my bottle of Cutty Sark?"

"Yes, Tom, and I am sorry. I will buy you another bottle. I promise."

This was so unexpected, Lepski dragged his tie down and released the collar button on his shirt.

"Okay. So what happened?"

"She got out her crystal ball and she seemed to go into a trance." Carroll put her hands to her eyes and released a long, exhausted sigh. Lepski wasn't the only one who could be a show-off. "I really think the poor old dear was a bit tiddly."

"Hold it. Did she get out her goddamn crystal ball before or after she got at my Cutty Sark?"

"Well, she does need a little stimulant before she can read the future."

"So she banged back half the bottle, huh?"

"A little more than half. Anyway, she talked a lot of rubbish. She said on no account were we to go on this trip. She said I must cancel all my arrangements and stay home. She said we would meet dangerous people and there was a woman named Catherine who would cause us a lot of trouble. She wasn't sure about the name. She said she couldn't see clearly. The crystal ball was misty."

Lepski released a snort that would have startled a bison.

"I bet it was. I would be misty too if I had knocked back more than half of a bottle of Scotch."

"I am a little worried, Tom. Mehitabel has always been

right in the past. Do you think we should go? Should we cancel the trip?"

Lepski recalled his bragging, bending Beigler's and Jacoby's ears back. They would laugh themselves silly if he backed out of a de luxe European trip. What excuse could he make?

He got up and went over to Carroll and patted her gently.

"Forget it, baby. The old sot was drunk. She was trying to keep you here. Who else gives her a bottle of Cutty Sark?"

"But it does worry me, Tom. What does she mean about a woman named Catherine? That we would meet dangerous people? I asked her and asked her, but she just sat there, moaning and shaking her head."

Lepski patted her again.

"Forget it! We're going to have the greatest vacation of our lives! Now, come on, baby, forget that old rum-dum. We're going to have a ball!" Seeing Carroll relaxing, he smiled hopefully, then asked, "What's for dinner?"

Ed Haddon paid off a taxi outside a modest motor hotel on the highway leading to Washington's downtown area. He was dressed conservatively in a dark business suit and he carried a briefcase. He paused to look at the balcony leading to the entrance to the hotel, but not seeing the man he had come to meet, he walked up the path, heading for the hotel's lobby.

"Ed!"

A soft voice made him pause and look sharply at an elderly clergyman who was sitting on the balcony and smiling at him.

This clergyman appeared to be in his late sixties with a round, pink-and-white face, wispy white hair and a benign smile that would attract children and elderly ladies. He was heavily built: the body of a man who liked his food and of medium height. He wore half-moon glasses. Kindness and Christianity oozed from him with the gentleness of a saint.

Haddon stared suspiciously, then he said in a hard, cold voice, "Were you speaking to me?"

The clergyman laughed: a nice, mellow sound that would cheer the faithful.

"Is it as good as that, Ed?" he asked.

"Jesus!" Haddon moved forward and stared. "That you, Lu?"

"Who else? Not bad, huh?"

Haddon stared again, then moved on to the balcony.

"It's really you?"

The clergyman nodded and patted a chair by his side.

"Good God!" Haddon said. "It's marvellous! What an artist!"

"Well, yes, you can say that. It's my best so far. I got your message. So, the deal's on?"

Haddon sat down, still staring at the clergyman. He had worked with Lu Bradey for the past ten profitable years. Bradey was the best art thief in the business, and, what was more important, he had never been caught, and had no police record. Apart from his expertise with any lock, he was a master of disguise. To look at him now: fat, benign, elderly, no one would imagine he was only thirty-five years of age, and as thin as a stick of asparagus. His facial skin was like rubber: a few pads inside his mouth and his lean face turned to fat. By wearing a padded waistcoat, he appeared solid. A wig, made by himself, gave him baldness and wispy white hair. Haddon had seen him in various disguises, but none of them as successful as this: an elderly, fat, kindly man of the church.

"Lu, you are a marvel," Haddon said. "I mean it!"

"Sure. I know I am. We go ahead?"

"Yes. Kendrick has found a buyer."

Bradey grimaced.

"That fat fag? Why not Abe? I like working with Abe."

"Abe's run out of money. There's a problem with Kendrick, but we'll get to that."

"I have problems too," Bradey said. "I spent yesterday morning at the museum. The security there is tighter than a mouse's ass-hole."

Haddon eyed him.

"Worry you?"

"Look, Ed, this is easily the toughest operation we have pulled. I'm relying on you. The museum is swarming with cops, guards, and worse, five bastards from the KGB. I went there in another disguise. I had to go through a scanner. The scanner picked up my car keys: it's that sensitive. There was a goddamn queue of people who had to leave everything they were carrying in the lobby: bags, umbrellas, canes, briefcases and so on. It took time. All this high security doesn't stop them from going: it adds to the excitement. Now, this icon you want. It's in a glass case and electrically wired. Touch the damn case and an alarm goes off. There is a heavy cord around it, keeping the gawpers back two feet. Touch the cord and a guard moves in. Pretending I wanted a closer look, I pressed against the cord and two tough guards snarled at me. Believe me, this is a tough one."

"Suppose there was no alarm and no guards, Lu, could you open the glass case?"

Lu chuckled.

"The lock is for the birds. Of course I could."

"So, we cut off the alarm. I've got that fixed. We do the job on Tuesday. Fifteen minutes before you arrive, two City electricians will be on the job. I have them lined up. The electrical feed-in wires are in the grounds of the museum. All these two have to do is to lift a trap and cut a cable. With the crowd going into the museum, who's going to bother with a couple of electricians in uniform? Okay, suppose one of the guards gets nosey? My two men can handle him. They are smooth operators and will have a forged permit. So, the alarm is out of action. Okay, so far?"

"If you say so, Ed, it is so."

"Right. These Vietnamese? Have you got them lined up?"

"Yes: thirty-five refugees are arriving by coach to see the wonders of the Hermitage exhibition," Bradey said with a sly smile. "Me, as the Reverend Samuel Hardcastle, bought the tickets, alerted the museum creeps and hired a coach . . . no problem there."

Haddon took from his briefcase a flat object.

"I've spent money getting this made, Lu. It's a smoke bomb, made of plastic. It'll go through the scanner without trouble. There's a switch. All you have to do is push the switch and you'll get a hell of a lot of smoke: enough smoke to blot out the first floor of the gallery. Now, imagine: the

32

gallery gets filled with smoke. There will be a panic. Guards rushing here and there, people screaming and rushing for the exits. While this is going on, you get the glass case open and grab the icon. I'm getting you a replica. You replace the icon with the replica, relock the case, and you're home."

Bradey leaned back in his chair while he thought.

Finally, he said, "No. Sorry, Ed, this won't do. First, the bomb. These security creeps are right on the ball. This bomb is bulky. I can't put it in my pocket. It would be spotted at once. Then the replica: someone carrying it would also be spotted. Someone carrying out the original would again be spotted even if there was a panic on. No, I don't like it."

Haddon smiled.

"Of course, but you haven't thought of a factor I have thought of. Smart as you are, I am smarter. Now, tell me what is the most sacred thing men, including security guards, respect?"

Bradey shrugged.

"I'd say a bottle of Scotch."

"You are wrong. The answer is a pregnant woman: a lovely looking woman about to give birth to a lovely, bouncing baby."

Bradey stiffened.

"Have you gone out of your mind, Ed?"

"You remember Joey Luck?"

"Sure. He was the best dip in the business. I hear he's retired."

"Right. I'm borrowing a trick of his. His daughter used to strap an egg shaped wicker basket on her tummy and put on a maternity gown. Joe and she then went to some self-service store and filched. She filled the basket with food. It was a beautiful idea and it never failed. So, in your party, you will want two nice-looking girls who appear to be pregnant: one of them will carry the smoke bomb, the other the replica, in baskets strapped to their tums. The original icon will go out the same way . . . like it?"

Bradey closed his eyes and thought. Haddon watched him, smiling. Then Bradey opened his eyes and grinned.

"Ed!" he said, keeping his voice low. "Goddamn it!

33

You're a genius! I love it!"

"Okay. How about the girls? They'll have to be in on this. Any ideas?"

"No problem. Among the party are two Viet whores who would slit their mothers' throats if the money was big enough." Bradey regarded Haddon. "This is going to cost, Ed. I'll have to bribe them with five grand apiece."

"So, okay. I'm not quibbling about costs. This is the big deal. Now, let's look at Kendrick's problem. He has to deliver the icon in Zurich, Switzerland."

Bradey flinched.

"That's his problem . . . and what a goddamn problem! Once the icon goes missing . . ."

"I know all that, and so does he. To get the icon into Switzerland is a big, big problem. No icon in Zurich, no money for him, nor you, nor me. That's it, Lu, so we'll have to help him. He's smart and he's working on it. If he doesn't come up with a safe idea, the operation is off."

Bradey shook his head.

"He can't do it, Ed. We might as well call if off now. Mind you, if we can sit on the icon for six months until the heat cools off . . ."

"It has to be delivered ten days after the steal."

Bradey shrugged.

"That's not possible. The security . . ."

"I know, but Kendrick may come up with an idea. He's a smart cookie. Let us assume he does. I want you to be in Zurich to take delivery of the money. Two million for me: one for you. Okay?"

"Man! He'll have to come up with a very smart idea, but, if he does, the deal is fine with me."

"Right. Now let us assume we can get the icon to Zurich, so we'll now go into details." Haddon dipped into his briefcase and produced a plan of the first floor of the Fine Arts, museum where the Hermitage exhibition was on display.

The two men moved closer as they began to study the plan.

For the past years, Carroll Lepski often paused outside *Maverick*, the best and most fashionable couturier in the city. She

34

would spend some time looking enviously at the display of elegant dresses and furs in the windows, then like Lepski staring at the display of choice cuts at Eddies, she would sigh and pass on.

But this morning, Carroll had money to spend, and she walked into the shop, her heart racing with excitement.

She found herself in a large room, furnished with antiques, with tapestry-covered chairs and several modern paintings of considerable value on the walls. At a large antique desk sat a middle-aged woman so elegantly dressed that Carroll paused.

The woman rose to her feet. Her dark eyes ran over Carroll, observing her linen dress, her elderly shoes and her plastic handbag.

The shop was owned by Roger Maverick who was Claude Kendrick's cousin. The antiques and paintings were loaned to him by Kendrick who changed them every six months.

Maverick had instilled into his staff the following axiom: *Never judge a sausage by its overcoat.*

Lucille had for years worked with Dior in Paris. Now forty-eight years of age, she had settled in Paradise City, respecting Maverick's genius for clothes and the enormous market opportunities among the rich women who swarmed into the city during the season.

Bearing in mind Maverick's axiom, she gave Carroll a gracious smile, wondering if this good-looking woman, rather shabbily dressed was just another time-waster.

"Madam?"

Carroll was never intimidated. She had decided what approach she should use, knowing her appearance in this lush-plush shop would be against her. She came to the point with a directness that startled Lucille.

"I am Mrs Tom Lepski," Carroll announced. "My husband is a first grade detective attached to the city's force. I have inherited money. We are going to Europe. I need a wardrobe. I don't intend to spend more than seven thousand dollars. What about it?"

This was still the dead season. Seven thousand dollars was not to be sniffed at, Lucille thought, and she widened her smile.

"Of course, Mrs Lepski. I am sure we can find you something suitable for your trip. Do please sit down. Mr Maverick will be delighted to discuss your needs with you, and make suggestions. Excuse me."

As Carroll sat down, Lucille took the plush elevator to the first floor where she found Maverick draping a bored-looking girl with a dress length.

Roger Maverick was tall, lean and extremely handsome. Around fifty-five years of age, he was not only a dress designer of considerable talent, a homosexual, but also a secret dealer in stolen furs, a very profitable sideline.

Lucille told him that the wife of Detective Lepski was below, seeking a wardrobe.

Maverick knew of every detective on the city's force, and he knew Lepski was the most dangerous. His lean, handsome face lit up.

"She appears to have inherited money and will spend seven thousand dollars," Lucille continued.

"Splendid! Now listen, my dear, she is to have the VIP treatment. Take her to the Washington room. Make her comfortable. Champagne . . . you know the thing. I will come along in ten minutes. In the meantime, find out her colours, and what she has in mind."

"Seven thousand dollars," Lucille said scornfully.

"Yes, yes; just do what I say, my dear."

With a slight shrug, Lucille took the elevator to the ground floor.

"Mr Maverick will be with you in a few minutes, Mrs Lepski. Please come with me."

Carroll followed her into the elevator and to the first floor. She followed her down a long corridor carpeted in red to a door. Opening the door, Lucille stood aside and motioned Carroll in.

The room was elegantly furnished with some more of Kendrick's antiques.

"Do sit down, Mrs Lepski. Perhaps a glass of champagne while we discuss what you require?"

A neatly dressed maid appeared with a silver tray on which stood an ice bucket containing a bottle of champagne and two glasses.

"You understand that I am not spending more than seven thousand dollars," Carroll said firmly. This VIP treatment made her uneasy.

"Of course, Mrs Lepski." Lucille poured the wine, handed Carroll a glass and sat down. "Now tell me please what you have in mind."

Three hours later, Carroll left the shop, walking on air.

She thought Roger Maverick the nicest, the most understanding, brilliant man she had ever met. She was now satisfied that she was equipped for the exciting trip to Europe. She had quickly realised that Maverick knew exactly what would suit her, and after a hesitant beginning, she relaxed and let him choose for her.

When the choice had been settled, she had begun to worry. Everything was so elegant that she couldn't imagine what it would cost.

"Not more than seven thousand," she said firmly when Maverick, beaming at her, asked if she was contented.

"Mrs Lepski, this is our dead season. Frankly, what you have chosen, in the season, would cost something around twenty thousand dollars. Frankly again, I have had these lovely clothes for some little time. Unhappily, I do not always have the opportunity of dressing a lady with a figure like yours. Usually, my clients are inclined to be stout. These are model dresses. I am only too happy to let you have them below half price. In fact, I will offer them to you for five thousand dollars which will allow you to have shoes and handbags to go with them."

"Why, that's marvellous!" Carroll had exclaimed.

"So happy you are happy. May I ask you to come here the day after tomorrow so my fitter can make a few minor alterations? I will have a selection of handbags and shoes for you to choose from."

As Maverick was a late riser, he took a late lunch, and invariably lunched at the Arts Club. There he found Claude Kendrick eating a breast of chicken in a heavy cream and mushroom sauce. Maverick sat at the same table and the two men exchanged smiles of greeting.

"How's business?" Kendrick asked, spearing a potato.

"Slow, but the season hasn't as yet begun." Maverick

37

ordered twelve blue-point oysters. "You are getting too fat, dear Claude. You should never eat potatoes."

Kendrick sighed and speared another potato.

"Louis is always nagging me, but I have to keep up my strength."

"I had an unexpected client this morning," Maverick said. "Mrs Tom Lepski, the cop's wife."

Kendrick's face darkened. He had had several unpleasant interviews with Lepski whom he considered an uncouth bully.

"What on earth did *she* want?"

"Apparently she has come into money, and they are going to Europe for a vacation. I've kitted her out. She has a nice figure. I got rid of some of my model stuff that has been hanging fire. She spent some five thousand dollars."

Kendrick looked longingly at another potato, then decided he mustn't waste this delicious sauce. He began to mash the potato.

"Very nice. Europe?"

"The usual tourist circuit: Paris, Monte Carlo, Montreux."

Kendrick's fork, loaded with chicken, potato and sauce, hovered before his open mouth. His little eyes turned cloudy. He lowered the fork.

"They are going to Switzerland?"

"She says so. She wants to see the mountains. I told her she should also go to Gstaad."

"And Lepski goes with her?"

"Of course." Maverick regarded his fat cousin. "What's on your mind?"

The oysters arrived.

"I don't know yet." Kendrick gobbled the food on his fork, then pushed back his chair. "I'll leave you to enjoy those delicious-looking oysters. Meet me in the lounge for coffee."

"But you haven't finished your lunch."

"It is time I began to think of my weight," and Kendrick plodded out of the restaurant and into the big, half-empty lounge.

Half an hour later, Maverick joined him.

38

"Luggage, Roger," Kendrick said as Maverick sat down by his side. "Mrs Lepski must have smart luggage to go with her purchases."

"She is a little stubborn about money," Maverick said. "Still, it is an idea. I'll see if I can persuade her."

Kendrick laid his fat hand on Maverick's arm.

"She must have luggage: a nice suitcase and a vanity box. In fact, dear Roger had better provide two suitcases: one for her and one for her husband, but the vanity box is a *must*."

Maverick studied his cousin.

"I rather doubt . . ."

"Wait. You will offer these pieces of luggage at such a ridiculously low price, she won't be able to resist. I will pay the difference."

"You are not being frank with me, Claude," Maverick said, his voice sharp. "You are cooking up something."

"Yes." Kendrick sighed. He knew his cousin. "Let us say I will pay you ten thousand dollars, and no questions asked."

"I am sorry, Claude. I will want to know what all this is about. I refuse to be involved in something you are hatching, unless I know exactly what it is."

Kendrick sighed again. He knew he would get no co-operation from his cousin without laying his cards face up. His sudden inspiration *had* to be the solution of getting the icon to Switzerland. The icon, carried by a well-known police officer, surely would cross the frontiers.

Knowing it would now cost him a great deal of money, he told Maverick of the big steal.

three

For the next two days, Carroll was extremely busy and loving every minute. She took Lepski to Harry Levine, one of the better tailors in the city, and supervised his kitting out for the trip. Lepski had flamboyant tastes, but Carroll would have none of it. She chose a charcoal-grey suit for evening wear, a sports outfit, a pair of extra dark blue slacks, four conservative shirts and three conservative ties. Although Lepski argued, she stamped on his objections, announcing that if he wanted that godawful shirt he kept fingering, then he would pay for it himself.

Finally, satisfied her husband would travel as a suitably dressed escort, she told Harry Levine to deliver the purchases and she paid by cheque.

"I need a new hat," Lepski said. "Got to have a hat."

"Lepski!" Carroll snapped. "Only cops and old, bald men wear hats these days! You don't need a hat! I don't want you to look like a cop!"

"Goddamn it! I *am* a cop!" Lepski shouted.

"No hat!" Carroll said firmly, "and if you dare to take that abortion you are now wearing on your head, I'll destroy it! Now, go back to work. I'm going to have my fitting."

Leaving Lepski muttering to himself, she walked the two blocks to Maverick.

She had a dreamy two hours with two fitters who pinned and smoothed and murmured compliments about her figure. To Carroll, this was living! Finally, the fitters told her the dresses and the travelling suit would be delivered in two days' time.

Leaving the fitting room, Carroll found Maverick waiting.

"Mrs Lepski! I *do* hope you are happy," he said with his wide, white toothy smile.

"Marvellous!" Carroll exclaimed. "I can't thank you enough!"

"Now the handbags and the shoes."

After another hour, guided by Maverick, Carroll bought three pairs of shoes and two handbags. She was nearly delirious with happiness.

Money! she thought. What it is to have money!

"Mrs Lepski, there is one other thing," Maverick said.

"Nothing more," Carroll said firmly. "I said seven thousand and I mean seven thousand."

"So far, you have spent six thousand, five hundred dollars," Maverick told her. "Have you thought about luggage? You and your husband will need smart-looking luggage when arriving in Paris. Alas, hotels judge people by their luggage no matter how well they are dressed. Have you thought of this?"

Carroll hadn't. She remembered the last time she and Lepski had gone on vacation what a sorry state their suitcases had been in. She remembered with a shudder Lepski's awful suitcase which he had inherited from his grandfather.

"Well, no. I hadn't thought . . . I suppose . . ."

At a signal from Maverick, one of his smartly dressed sales girls came in with two splendid-looking suitcases in dark blue leather with dark red bands.

"Now these cases have a little history," Maverick lied. "They were ordered by one of my very rich clients who is extremely difficult to please. I had them made specially for her and to her specifications. She returned them, complaining they were not large enough. We had a little argument." He paused to give Carroll his toothy smile. "Since she had ordered them, she paid for them and I made larger ones for her. So, Mrs Lepski, I can offer you these two magnificent

42

suitcases for one hundred dollars. What do you say?"

Carroll examined the suitcases. She thought they were the most beautiful suitcases she had ever seen, and she longed to possess them.

"But that is almost giving them away," she said.

"Well, not quite. I have been paid for them. I would like to do you a little favour."

Carroll didn't hesitate.

"It's a deal."

"How wise. Then, Mrs Lepski, I have a vanity box to match these two suitcases, and this I propose to offer you as a present. It is really rather nice."

The sales girl produced the vanity box. When Carroll saw how it was fitted, she could only gape at it.

"You mean you are *giving* it to me?"

"Why not? It's been paid for and your kind order deserves a slight return. Please accept it."

"Why, thank you! It's just marvellous!"

"I will deliver the dresses and the cases to you on Wednesday. I understand you will be leaving on Thursday."

"Oh, I can take them with me." Carroll was reluctant to be parted from her purchases.

"Please, Mrs Lepski. I would like to put your initials and Mr Lepski's initials on the cases. I would also like to furbish the vanity box with our special selection of cosmetics. Do leave it to me."

"I can't thank you enough, Mr Maverick. Then Wednesday?"

"Without fail, Mrs Lepski," and Maverick escorted her to the elevator.

Three minutes later, he was speaking to Kendrick on the telephone.

"No problem, dear Claude," he said. "She is happy with the suitcases, and I have promised to deliver them and the vanity box Wednesday morning."

"Splendid!" Kendrick exclaimed. "The object is eight inches by nine and half an inch thick."

"I will personally dismantle the vanity box. The object, of course, will add to the weight, but not unduly."

"Yes. That is a small problem."

43

"She didn't pick the box up. She won't know the difference. I plan to fill the box with our most deluxe cosmetics.
She will be dazzled by the contents. Even if the box weighed
a hundredweight, she wouldn't be parted from it."

"Splendid work, Roger."

"You owe me three thousand dollars, Claude."

Kendrick sighed.

"Yes."

"And one hundred thousand when the object is paid for."

Again Kendrick sighed.

"Yes."

"Good. Send Louis to me Tuesday evening. 'Bye now,"
and Maverick hung up.

Kendrick replaced the receiver, took off his wig and pol-
ished his bald head with his silk handkerchief. Then slapping
the wig on anyhow, he called for Louis.

There was a delay as Louis was engaged with a client,
but twenty minutes later, he slid into Kendrick's office.

"The replica, chéri," Kendrick said. "Is it ready?"

"Of course . . . a beautiful job." Louis looked uneasily at
Kendrick. "This is dreadfully dangerous, baby. It really has
me worried."

"Bring it to me!" Kendrick snapped. He was far from
being happy about this operation, but he kept reminding
himself of the three-million-dollar profit.

When Louis returned with the replica of the icon, Kendrick's confidence rose.

"You are a craftsman, chéri," he said. "This is very good."

He carefully compared the replica with the illustration of
the original.

"I couldn't match the colours exactly," Louis said, "but
it is near enough."

"Yes . . . near enough."

"Do be careful what you are doing, baby," Louis said.
"There will be a horrid uproar. We could land in jail."

Kendrick silently agreed, but he put the replica in his
briefcase, straightened his wig and made for the door.

"Relax, chéri. Think of the money you will be making."

He left the Gallery and drove to the Spanish Bay hotel

where he found Ed Haddon sunning himself on the terrace.

"Let us go to your apartment, Ed," Kendrick said after the two men had shaken hands.

In Haddon's luxury apartment, the door closed and locked, Kendrick produced the replica.

"Your man is good," Haddon said, taking the replica and examining it. "This is just what I want."

"Let us sit down. I have found a possible solution to get the original to Switzerland. If this doesn't work, nothing will. There is a risk, of course, but I think a minor one," Kendrick said as he sat down in a comfortable chair.

Haddon grinned and rubbed his hands.

"I felt sure you would come up with an idea, Claude. How is it to be done?"

"First, you are certain you can get the icon?"

Haddon sat by Kendrick's side.

"Don't let's waste time. I said you will have the icon Tuesday," Haddon said irritably. "You'll have it! How do you get it to Switzerland?"

Kendrick told him about his cousin, Roger Maverick.

"By the sheerest luck, the wife of a police officer came to Roger's shop to buy clothes. She has inherited money. She and her husband, Lepski, are going to Europe on vacation. They go to Paris, Monte Carlo and Switzerland. This means they will go through the French and Swiss customs controls. My cousin has sold her suitcases and a vanity box. My cousin will take the vanity box to pieces, insert the icon and put the box together again. What do you think?"

Haddon stared at him.

"You mean you are using a cop to smuggle the icon out?"

Kendrick nodded.

"What better and safer person? Who would suspect a first grade detective on vacation smuggling the icon out of the country? Lepski is well known to the customs' officials at Miami airport. They will wave him through. He has only to show his shield for the French and the Swiss officials also to wave him through. Do you like the idea?"

Haddon brooded for a long minute, then grinned.

"Looks like you and I, Claude, are going to make a great

deal of money. I love the idea!"

"Yes." Kendrick shifted uneasily, "but there are still problems."

Haddon gave him a sharp look.

"What problems?"

"We are handing Lepski's wife six million dollars, Ed," Kendrick said. "Of course, she doesn't realize that, but nevertheless, she will have charge of six million dollars. I know nothing about her. She may be a pea-brain. She may be one of these women who leave things behind, lose things, forget things. Suppose she left the vanity box somewhere? You follow my thinking?"

"She would leave her pants behind, but she's not going to leave a valuable vanity box behind."

"All the same . . . women do do awful things like even leaving their diamonds behind."

Haddon nodded.

"You're right. Okay, Claude, I'll fix it." He looked at his watch. "I'll fly up to Washington and talk to Bradey. We must arrange for someone to be with the Lepskis until they reach Switzerland. Bradey will take care of that."

Kendrick relaxed.

"That's it, Ed. Someone who will never let her or Lepski out of his sight, but warn Bradey that Lepski is a smart cop. They will have to be tailed with care."

"Leave it to me. I'll personally deliver the icon to your Gallery around five o'clock Tuesday and I will let you know what I have arranged. Don't worry, Claude, this is going to work."

Four hours later, Haddon was talking to Lu Bradey, still disguised as a clergyman. They were sitting together in Bradey's motor hotel room.

Bradey nodded approval when he heard of Kendrick's plan to smuggle the icon to Switzerland.

"That's real smart," he said.

Then Haddon explained Kendrick's fears.

"This is where we have to help, Lu," he said. "I will check that the Lepskis get through the Miami customs. When they reach Paris we will need someone to tail them and stick with them, making sure the vanity box remains in their possession. Any ideas?"

Bradey thought, then nodded.

"No problem. Pierre and Claudette Duvine. They are my French agents and smart. You can leave this to me, Ed. It'll cost, of course, but they will stick to the Lepskis like glue all the way through the Swiss frontier."

"Sure?"

Bradey smiled.

"My dear Ed!"

Haddon nodded, satisfied.

In a comfortably furnished duplex-apartment on rue Alfred Bruneau in the 16th arrondissement, Paris, Pierre Duvine was counting the remaining money he had in his wallet, and in the world.

Duvine, dark, around thirty-seven years of age, was often mistaken for Alain Delon, the French movie actor. He was an expert in antiques, jewellery and 18th-century paintings. Working on a profitable commission, he kept Lu Bradey informed of sound, possible steals.

As everyone knows, Paris is a dead city during the month of August. It was only just coming alive in this first week in September. Even now, there were plenty of parking places, and the best restaurants were only just beginning to stretch their limbs for yet another profitable season.

Usually, Pierre and his wife spent August in the Midi where the action was, but Pierre had had an unpleasant motoring accident, and was only just out of hospital. Claudette, his wife, who was devoted to him, had stayed in their Paris apartment so she could visit him in hospital every day.

He fingered the bank notes and frowned.

Claudette came in from the bathroom.

"Money?" she asked, looking at the bank notes Pierre was fingering.

Claudette, five years younger than Pierre, even at ten o'clock in the morning, even having just rolled out of bed, presented a charming picture. She was tall, slender, with Venetian red hair and emerald-green eyes. Long legged with

47

a superb, lithesome body, she played an important part in Duvine's machinations. Time and again, she had sexed some rich old man into inviting her to his home, noted with expertise anything worth stealing, allowed the old man to take her to bed, then returning home, gave Pierre a detailed description of the articles worth stealing, the kind of locks, the alarm system and so on. This information was passed to Lu Bradey who then organized the steal.

The Duvines had been happily married now for five years, and although there were times when Pierre was moody, and sometimes bad tempered, Claudette, recognizing the signs, soothed and sexed him into a good mood. Not once had they quarrelled, due to Claudette's calming influence.

"We are getting short of cash," Pierre said gloomily. "After paying that awful hospital bill, we'll be down to practically nothing."

Claudette stroked his face lovingly.

"Never mind, my treasure, something always turns up. Give me five minutes, and I'll have coffee for you."

Pierre patted her bottom and smiled.

"Sugar, you are my heart and my life."

She ran off to the bedroom while Pierre recounted his money. He had a little over ten thousand francs. He grimaced. Among his many talents, he was an expert pickpocket. Since working with Lu Bradey, he had dropped dipping into pockets, but maybe, he thought uneasily, he would have to begin again until the rich returned to Paris. He didn't like the thought. There was always a risk, and he was out of practice.

As Claudette brought in a tray with coffee, the telephone bell rang.

They looked at each other.

"Now, who can this be?" Pierre got to his feet. He lifted the receiver. "Pierre Duvine," he announced.

"This is ·Lu Bradey." The voice came clearly over the trans-Atlantic line. "I'm in Washington. I have a job for you. Meet me at the Charles de Gaulle Hilton bar at 23.30 tonight. Bring Claudette," and the line went dead.

"Bradey!" Pierre exclaimed, beaming at Claudette. "A job!"

Both of them knew, when working with Bradey, the money was always good.

"See, my treasure?" Claudette cried, setting down the coffee tray. "I said something would turn up," and she threw herself into Pierre's arms.

At exactly 23.30, Pierre and Claudette walked into the crowded Hilton bar. They looked around and found no one resembling Lu Bradey until a hand touched Pierre's arm. Turning, he found a small, insignificant-looking business man, wearing a beard and moustache, his complexion sallow, his half-moon glasses at the end of his nose, at his side.

Both the Duvines were used to Bradey's many disguises, but for a moment, the disguise was so good, they hesitated.

"We'll go to my room," Bradey said quietly.

Nothing was said until they reached the third floor, and Bradey unlocked the door of his room. Once inside, Pierre said, "You are fantastic, Lu."

"Of course." Bradey waved Claudette to the only arm chair, waved Pierre to an upright chair and sat on the bed. "I have an urgent and important job for you two. Now, listen carefully."

With no mention of the icon, Bradey told them that they had to remain in constant touch with Tom and Carroll Lepski as soon as they arrived at Charles de Gaulle airport on this coming Friday.

"They are doing Paris, then Monte Carlo and the Midi, then going on to Switzerland," he told them. "Your job is to stick closer to them than a baby to its mother's tit. The woman will be carrying a vanity box. In this box, unknown to either of them, will be an object that has to reach Switzerland. It will be built into the box and I don't anticipate any trouble with the customs, but it is your job to see the woman does carry it through the Swiss customs."

Pierre's expression became thoughtful.

"What is the object?"

"That you needn't know, but it is valuable."

"Not drugs?"

"Of course not! It is an objet d'art."

Pierre and Claudette exchanged glances.

49

"Doesn't sound difficult. What's in it for us?" Pierre asked.

"Twenty thousand Swiss francs, and all expenses paid," Bradey said, who had been doing calculations on the flight to Paris. "You can regard this job as a paid vacation."

"Let's get this clear," Pierre said who was cautious when dealing with Bradey. "We are to follow these two, stay at the same hotels, make sure the woman always leaves with her vanity box when they move to another hotel, and when they pass through the Swiss customs, we get paid twenty thousand Swiss francs. Right?"

Bradey stroked his false beard.

"A little more than that, Pierre. You will stay with them at their Swiss hotel. You will take the box when they are out of the room and bring it to me at the Eden hotel, Zurich, and I will pay you off."

"Who are these people?" Claudette asked.

"A good question. Yes, you must know. The man is a first grade detective attached to the Paradise City, Florida, police force. She is his wife."

Pierre stiffened.

"Are you telling me I am to steal a vanity box from the wife of a top-class cop?"

"What's wrong with that?"

"Plenty. As soon as the box is missing, the cop will raise hell. I don't like this, Lu."

Bradey smiled.

"Relax. He won't know it has been taken."

"But his wife will," Claudette said sharply.

"Neither of them will. I have arranged for an exact replica of the box to be made and I will deliver it to you in Switzerland. All you have to do, Pierre, is to get into their room while they are out, open Mrs Lepski's vanity box, put her personal stuff into the replica, then walk out with the original box. Neither Lepski nor his wife will have an idea the boxes have been switched."

Duvine considered this, then nodded.

"Nice idea. Okay, let's go further into this. Where will they be staying? In Paris and in Monaco, you just can't get a room without a reservation. If we are to stay at their hotels,

50

I must know in which hotel to book."

"I have that covered." Bradey took from his wallet a folded sheet of paper. "Ed worked it. Kendrick's cousin went to the American Express in Paradise City and told the girl who is handling the Lepski's trip that he wanted to send flowers to each hotel where they stop. She gave him a copy of their itinerary. They stay at the Excelsior hotel, Paris, for four days, the Metropole hotel in Monaco for three days, and at the Montreux Palace, Montreux for three days. You will switch boxes at the Palace hotel. Here are the dates," and he handed Pierre the sheet of paper.

"Twenty thousand Swiss francs and all expenses?"

"Yes."

Claudette gave an ecstatic sigh.

Pierre studied the itinerary. After a few moments, he looked at Bradey with a smile.

"I have an idea. Suppose we happen to be at Charles de Gaulle when the Lepskis arrive. Suppose Claudette gets chatting with the Lepskis, then I arrive. Staying at the Excelsior? What a coincidence? We are staying there too, then we are driving to Monaco. My car's outside. Let's all go together to the Excelsior. I know Americans. I assure you by the time we get to the Excelsior, we will be old friends. Americans want to be loved. I will then offer to show them Paris, then drive them down to Monaco. I will be able to iron out all their problems with the luggage. This way we will never let the vanity box out of our sight. What do you think?"

"I like it, but be careful of Lepski. He's a cop."

"Yes. Now how about some money, Lu?" Pierre said. "I'm short."

Bradey took out his wallet.

As Gustav Holtz was packing documents in a briefcase, Herman Radnitz came in.

"You are to see Kendrick and find out from him exactly how he is proposing to smuggle the icon to Zurich and who his confederates are. Don't stand any nonsense with him. Unless I am convinced he can get the icon to Zurich, I will drop the business."

"Yes, sir," Holtz said. "I will go now."

51

"Wait." Radnitz lit a cigar. "I need a replacement for Lu Silk."

For a brief moment, Holtz's eyes narrowed.

Lu Silk had been Radnitz's hired killer: a ruthless hit-man who removed people who threatened to upset Radnitz's various deals. Only a few months ago, Silk had been killed while working on an operation in which Radnitz was not implicated.*

From long experience, Radnitz had discovered that Holtz invariably came up with an immediate solution for many of his problems, but he was surprised when Holtz nodded.

"Certainly, sir . . . my nephew."

"Your nephew? Explain yourself."

"My brother and his wife were killed in a motoring accident. Their son, Sergas, then aged three, survived. As his only relation, I arranged his upbringing," Holtz said quietly. "He has had an excellent education. He speaks fluent English, French, German and Russian. At the age of eighteen, against my wishes, he became a mercenary soldier. I lost contact with him for some ten years, then one day, he came to me. He was bored with the Army and wondered if I could do something for him. He reminded me so much of Lu Silk, that I have been financing him in case Silk ever disappointed you or was killed as he has been. Sergas has all the qualifications you need, sir. I guarantee him."

"You are a remarkable man, Holtz," Radnitz said. "You appear always to look ahead for my requirements. What is your nephew doing now?"

"Improving his technique in arms, and waiting to serve you."

"Very well. Since you guarantee him, he can consider himself hired on the same terms as I hired Silk. Now, go and talk to Kendrick."

Half an hour later, Gustav Holtz was sitting in Claude Kendrick's room. Kendrick, flustered by Holtz's macabre appearance and alarmed to hear that Radnitz might, at the last moment, pull out of their agreement, explained to Holtz how the icon was to be smuggled to Switzerland. He also

---

* See: *Consider Yourself Dead.*

gave Holtz details about Haddon, Bradey and Duvine.

Holtz listened, then he said, "This vanity box. I will need a photograph of it to show Mr Radnitz."

"That is no problem. I have photographed it for the replica," Kendrick said and produced a series of coloured photographs.

"I feel sure Mr Radnitz will approve of your planning," Holtz said, rising to his feet. "I congratulate you."

"So I may expect payment in Zurich?" Kendrick asked, a little anxiously.

"When the icon is delivered, payment will be made."

Back at the Belvedere hotel, Holtz explained to Radnitz in detail Kendrick's plan.

Radnitz listened, and from time to time, nodded approval.

"Yes. It is a clever idea," he said after examining the photographs of the vanity box. Then his toad-like face turned vicious. "Ever since Kendrick failed when trying to get those Russian stamps, I promised myself to teach him a lesson. I want a replica of this box made. Your nephew is to bring it to my villa at Zurich."

Ever alert, Holtz said, "If you will excuse me, sir, that would not be wise."

Radnitz glared at him.

"Why not?"

"A young man carrying a lady's vanity box would be immediately suspect by the security people. He would have to pass through the Swiss customs. It would create dangerous difficulties. I know a man in Zurich who can make the box. All I have to do is to send him these photographs. I assure you there will be no problems."

Radnitz nodded.

"You seem to think of everything. Very well. I leave it to you. I expect your nephew at the end of the week."

Holtz inclined his head, took the photographs and went away.

The coloured girl moved in her sleep, releasing a soft moan of pleasure. She lay naked on the grey-white sheet on the bed, her slim body glistening with sweat, her long, black hair a silky shield across her face.

53

Her movement brought the man lying by her side awake with the awareness of a jungle cat.

He looked around the small sordid room, then at the girl sleeping at his side, then across the room to the rotting shutters that partially kept out the glare of Florida's sun. His eyes took in the cane stool, the chipped enamel basin on the rickety table, supported by bending bamboo legs, and to his sweat shirt, Levis and loafer shoes, dropped on the dusty rush mat as he had stripped off.

He half-turned and lifted himself on his elbow to look down at the girl, his eyes running over her body. He liked black meat. White women now bored him. They expected so much before they gave out, and even when he did go along with their stupid teasing and demands, there were times when they dodged the final issue. Black girls either meant business or said no. That he appreciated. Since coming to Miami, he had shunned the spoilt, vapid white girls and had hunted in West Miami where the action was.

At the age of twenty-eight, Sergas Holtz was a splendidly built male animal who took a fanatical pride in keeping his body in peak condition. Tall, with shoulder-length straw-coloured hair, boxer's muscles, long-legged, when seen from behind, he aroused female interest, but the interest became cautious when he turned.

Sergas Holtz's face scared, yet fascinated women. His face narrow, a short boxer's nose, small ice-cold grey eyes and a sensual mouth was a sexual challenge for girls who wanted excitement. Even when he laughed, his eyes remained mirthless. He was a man who didn't invite friendship. During the years, serving as a mercenary soldier, murdering, looting and raping with others in the Congo and other parts of Africa, none of his comrades took to him. Even, although an excellent student, none of his teachers were ever friendly, sensing uneasily that there was something evil in him.

Sergas preferred being a loner. When not fighting in the jungle, he spent hours in the Army gymnasium, boxing, learning karate and all the tricks the Army could teach him of the quick, silent kill.

TV Westerns fascinated him. He became the fastest gun

draw in the Army and the best marksman. Satisfied with his marksmanship, he turned his attention to knife fighting. He became an expert knife-thrower.

There was only one man with whom Sergas found he could talk frankly: his uncle, Gustav Holtz. Apart from the fun of killing ruthlessly and chasing women, Sergas's only other interest was money. Tired of Army life, he had returned from Africa to Paris where his uncle worked for Herman Radnitz. From what Sergas learned from his uncle, Radnitz impressed him. Radnitz's enormous wealth, his ruthless power, his association with the Heads of various governments made a big impact.

Sergas and his uncle had had a long discussion about his future. Sergas was inclined to join one of Castro's groups, and go to Cuba, but Gustav had counselled patience. He would supply Sergas with enough money to live on. Sooner or later, Gustav promised, he would find a place for him in the Radnitz kingdom. He told him about Lu Silk.

"Mr Radnitz has many enemies. Some of them a little too powerful. Silk is told, and the enemy dies. Silk is paid four thousand dollars a month as a retainer and for a successful disposal a lump sum of fifty thousand dollars. He is no longer young. He will either retire or be killed," Gustav said. "You could take his place. We must wait, but in the meantime perfect yourself," and he went on to tell Sergas of Lu Silk's qualifications.

"Why wait? Tell me where I can find this man and I'll get rid of him," Sergas said.

Gustav shook his head.

"Right now, you are not yet in Silk's class. You are very good, but he is perfection. I won't have you risking your life. Besides, Radnitz would be suspicious. Wait."

So Sergas remained in Paris, honing his killing technique, chasing girls and reading biographies of the world's leaders. When Radnitz moved to Paradise City, Sergas moved to Miami where he rented a modest one-room apartment. In Miami, he spent hours on the beach, swimming, jogging and keeping in trim, hunting girls and throwing knives at the palm trees.

He had faith in his uncle. Sooner or later, he would become a member of the Radnitz kingdom. If his uncle said so, it would be so.

This afternoon, he had needed a woman. He had gone to West Miami on his Honda motorcycle and to the black quarter. He had found this girl, now sleeping by his side. He had bought her a coke. She had told him her man was in Key West on business and wouldn't be back before the evening. They had looked at each other, and Sergas knew she meant action. Clinging to him on the Honda, she had directed him to a shack where she lived.

As soon as his lust was released, Sergas always lost interest in his sexual partners. He slid off the bed and put on his Levis. As he was reaching for his sweat shirt, he heard a car pull up with screeching brakes. Moving swiftly to a rotting shutter, he peered through the slats.

A battered, dusty Lincoln was before the shack. From it sprang a big black, wearing a cream-coloured suit and a panama hat. His brutal face with its fuzz of beard, shiny with sweat, was a vicious, frightening mask. He came storming up the path as the girl came awake. She sat up, her face turning grey with terror as the black flung his weight against the door.

Sergas looked at her as the door quaked under the shoulder impact. Screws from the lock flew into the room. An evil little smile flitted across his mouth. He moved swiftly against the wall to the left of the door. As he did so, the door burst open and the black, snarling, his knife blade flashing in the sunbeams coming through the shutters, rushed in.

The girl on the bed screamed, covering her breasts and cringing back.

Moving like a striking cobra, Sergas came from behind the door. The side of his open hand cut down òn the black's bull neck in a vicious karate chop.

The shack shook as the black went down like a pole-axed bull.

The girl screamed again.

"Relax," Sergas said. "Don't excite yourself."

"Is he dead?" The girl scrambled to the foot of the bed and peered down at the vast, inert body.

56

"No . . . no. Just asleep." Sergas put on his sweat shirt.

"When he wakes, he will kill me!"

Sergas bent to put on his loafers.

"No, he won't. I'll fix that for you."

"He'll beat me!" the girl moaned.

Sergas shook his head, his long hair like a yellow flag.

"He won't."

"He will! He'll beat me until I bleed!"

Sergas bent over the unconscious black, then taking one of the black's enormous hands, he fastened on to the little finger. With a quick jerk, he wrenched back the finger, breaking the bone. Taking the other hand, he again broke the little finger, then smiling at the girl, he said, "He won't be able to touch you now, baby. He'll be too sorry for himself, but just in case he feels like kicking you, I'll fix his feet."

As the girl stared in horror, her body shivering, Sergas pulled off the black's shoes and broke the two little toes of the black's enormous, stinking feet.

"You take care of him, baby. He'll be glad of your care." Then giving his mirthless smile, he walked out, got astride his Honda and roared off back to his Miami apartment.

As he entered the small shabby room, he saw the answering light on his telephone was glowing. The girl at the reception desk told him there was an urgent call for him and gave him a Paradise City number.

Sergas's eyes lit up.

His uncle!

He dialled the number.

"Sergas," he said when he heard his uncle's voice.

"Come immediately to the Belvedere hotel, Paradise City," his uncle said. "You are now a member of Mr Radnitz's staff," and he hung up.

Sergas replaced the telephone receiver. He stood still for a long moment, then began hurriedly to pack.

The long wait was over.

four

Fred Scooner, Head of the security guards, permanently attached to the Washington Fine Arts museum, stood at the head of the three broad flights of marble steps leading to the entrance lobby of the first floor where the Hermitage exhibits were on display.

Scooner, in his early fifties, was a bulky man, wearing a dark blue uniform with a peak cap. The gold braid on his cuffs indicated his rank.

By his side was FBI Agent Jack Trumbler, wearing a dark suit, bare-headed, his jacket bulging slightly, concealing the police special .38 he carried in a shoulder holster.

The two men were regarding the orderly queue of people as they waited to go through the security screen. A guard was posted at the entrance doors, regulating the flow of the queue. Another guard was directing people to a long counter where they handed in everything they happened to be carrying.

Trumbler, lean and hard-faced, in his early thirties, disliked this assignment. It wasn't his idea of action just to stand around and watch art-lovers and gawpers, but his instructions had been precise and clear. His boss had told him he and his four men must be continually on the alert.

"This goddamn city," his boss had said, "is full of nuts. The exhibits are all wired so the chances of a steal are remote, but a nut with a bottle of acid can do damage. I have it from the President himself that there must be no incidents, and it will be your ass in a sling if there is."

The same instructions from the White House had been passed to Fred Scooner. Every one of his men for the past week had been on key-alert, and the strain was beginning to tell. Even when the museum closed at 20.00, guards, in shifts, remained on duty throughout the night.

"I'll be glad when this shindig is over," Trumbler said. "One more week!"

Scooner nodded.

"These people look all right, but no one ever knows. There are so many anti-Russian cranks around. Someone politically motivated could try to damage one of these exhibits. I reckon the last week will be the most dangerous."

"You mean someone casing the joint, then returning?"

"That's my guess."

"If someone does do damage, there'll be one hell of a row," Trumbler said gloomily. "What a chance for the Soviets to claim we are irresponsible! It wouldn't surprise me if they would be happy if a nut did do something."

"The security is as tight as we can make it."

"Yeah. How do you get along with those KGB creeps?"

"No contact. They pretend they only speak Russian."

"Me too."

While the two men were talking and while a continuous stream of people moved up the museum's steps, in the grounds, more queues were forming.

A small blue van on which was painted *Washington City Electricity Corporation* pulled up at the entrance gates. A tall black, wearing the familiar Corporation's uniform, slid out of the van and went over to one of the guards.

"Mr Scooner phoned," he said. "You have trouble with your fuse box."

The guard eyed the black.

"You know where the fuse box is?"

"Sure." The black grinned. "Around the back."

The guard, seeing a big air-conditioned coach pull up, impatiently waved the black through. The van drove off around the back of the museum where there were no guards.

The guard moved to the coach. From it came a short, fat, beaming clergyman,

"Reverend Hardcastle," he said. "I have brought my flock to see the exhibition. It has been arranged, I believe."

The guard had been alerted that thirty-five Vietnamese refugees would be arriving in charge of a Reverend Hardcastle.

"Tickets, sir?" he said, saluting.

"Certainly." The fat clergyman produced a book of tickets and a passport.

The guard waved the passport aside.

"That isn't necessary, sir."

"I understood the security is very strict. I thought I should bring my passport."

Clergymen, fat or thin, were, in the guard's opinion, goddamn do-gooders and a nuisance. He checked the tickets, looked at the yellow faces peering down at him from the coach windows, snorted, then waved to the driver.

"Go ahead, sir," he said to the clergyman. "There's a security check in the lobby. Please tell your people to leave everything in the coach that they may be carrying. This will save time. Umbrellas, bags, canes and any metal objects."

"I understand. Thank you," and the clergyman returned to the coach which drove up to the entrance of the museum.

There was a delay before the passengers descended. There was confusion in the coach while they rid themselves of their possessions. The last two women out of the coach had to be assisted. They were both in advanced stages of pregnancy.

"Oh, hell!" Scooner muttered. "Look at this lot!"

He stared down at the group of Vietnamese; some men, some women, some with small children: all dressed in their national costume: the women in Cheong-sams, the men in white shirts and black trousers.

"Refugees," Scooner went on. "The padre organized this

61

outing through the Brotherhood of Love society."

"Look at those two women," Trumbler muttered. "They look as if they are about to drop their bundles any moment."

"I hope to God not!"

Below in the lobby, Chick Hurley, the guard on the entrance gates, was also staring at the two pretty Vietnamese girls, big with child.

Hurley, young, a little overweight, not over-bright, had opted to join the museum's security guards, knowing it would be a steady pensionable job that would suit his lack of ambition and his pace in life. Ten months ago, feeling his position secure, and with no extravagant tastes, he had got married. His wife was like him: without ambition, but desperately anxious to raise a family. They both loved children. His wife was also big with child, and the birth was expected any day. Hurley who doted on his fat wife was horrified by the way her body had expanded. He had seen a number of TV films depicting child birth and they had so upset him that during the past week he had been in torture, visualising what his wife was about to face. When he saw the two flower-like Vietnamese girls, he felt a chill run up his spine.

As the fat clergyman handed in the book of tickets, then moved to his group, Hurley left the entrance doors and approached him.

"There's an elevator, sir," he said to the clergyman. "These two ladies shouldn't climb those steps."

The clergyman beamed at him.

"How kind! How very thoughtful!"

Hurley smirked.

"Well, sir, I'm expecting my own any day now."

"Congratulations! Splendid!"

Hurley indicated the elevator and hurried back to his post at the entrance.

While the rest of the Vietnamese climbed the steps, the clergyman and the two pregnant girls entered the elevator. They waited for the others, then the clergyman said, "Follow me, please and do not stray," and he set off into the first room of the exhibition.

"Some of these Viets are attractive," Trumbler said. "I

wouldn't mind giving one or two of them a ride."

"Keep your mind on the job," Scooner snapped. "You take the right wing. I'll take the left. We'll circulate."

As the Vietnamese group moved from exhibit to exhibit, pausing to listen to the clergyman's remarks, Trumbler walked on, past the special alcove that housed the Catherine the Great icon which was not attracting much attention, and into the vast hall that housed some of the finest oil paintings in the world. Here, the crowd was dense, and he noted that all five members of the KGB were mingling with the crowd, and two of his own men were also watching.

The clergyman paused at one of the windows and looking down, he saw a small blue van leaving the grounds of the museum. He glanced at his watch, then he moved on to another exhibit. Ten minutes later, he paused in his talk and gave a slight nod of his head to one of the pregnant girls. She moved away from the group and approached a guard who was stifling a yawn. He had been on night duty and was anxiously waiting to be relieved.

"A toilet, sir?"

He eyed her and her inflated belly, then gave her a friendly smile.

"That door over there, miss."

"Thank you, sir."

The girl walked to a door on the far side of the icon's alcove as the fat clergyman led his group into the alcove.

"Now, here, my friends," he said, "is the first icon known and used by Catherine the Great of Russia."

The group made a complete circle around the roped off glass case.

A guard moved forward.

"Please keep clear of the ropes," he said curtly.

"Of course; of course," the clergyman said and opened the illustrated catalogue he was carrying. As the guard moved back, he went on, "The artist is unknown, but, as you can see, considering the vast age . . ."

There came a loud hissing sound and thick, black smoke billowed out from behind a large exhibit near the door of the lady's toilet.

The Vietnamese immediately panicked. The girls screamed and jostled each other. The men shouted and the children wailed.

The guard rushed in the direction of the smoke, but the smoke now was so dense, he staggered back, choking and coughing.

People in the hall of paintings also panicked. Cries of "FIRE!" resounded through the rooms. There was a concerted rush for the various exits.

Scooner, hearing the uproar, ran from the right wing and into dense, black smoke. This was no fire, he told himself: this was a powerful smoke bomb. He ran to the head of the steps and bawled down to Hurley who was gaping up at him.

"Shut the doors! No one in; no one out!"

The other guard on the entrance doors with Hurley took the steps three at a time and joined Scooner. They were nearly knocked down the steps by the screaming Vietnamese who were trying to rush down to the exit, but Scooner and the guard blocked them off.

"Stay right where you are!" Scooner barked. "There's no danger!"

Alone in the lobby, Hurley set his fat back against the closed entrance doors and gaped up the steps at the confusion going on above.

"My friend."

He started and turned to find the fat clergyman at his side. The elevator doors stood open, and one of the pregnant Vietnamese girls lay on the floor.

"I fear this disturbance has brought her to labour," the clergyman said. "Mr Scooner has been kind enough to telephone for an ambulance. Ah! I hear it coming. Please help!"

Had Hurley been less dim-witted, he would have realised that Scooner, battling with the Vietnamese at the head of the steps couldn't possibly have had time to telephone for an ambulance, but the dreadful moaning coming from the Vietnamese girl, and the shrill note of the siren of the approaching ambulance paralysed what wits he had. God! he thought, this could be happening to Meg in a day or so! He hurried with the clergyman to the girl, and together they both lifted her. Her face, glistening with sweat, was contorted with pain.

"Let the ambulance people in," the clergyman said sharply.

In a complete dither, Hurley ran to the doors, slid back the bolts and let in two black men, carrying a stretcher. He was not to know that these two men had but a quarter of an hour ago, been in the uniforms of the *Washington City Electricity Corporation*.

"We'll take care of her," the tallest of the blacks said. They scooped the girl on to the stretcher as she gave a wail of pain. Before Hurley, shuddering at the sound, had time to think, the two stretcher bearers were out, loading the stretcher into the ambulance, which went roaring down the drive with the siren at full blast.

"Splendid!" the clergyman exclaimed. "Thank you. Now, I must return to my flock. I can't think what is happening up there." He moved swiftly to the elevator and pressing the button to the second floor, waited until the elevator came to rest. People, and they were few, who had been looking at other exhibits on the second floor were gathered at the head of the steps. The clergyman entered one of the men's toilets and shut the door. Three minutes later, the door opened and a young, thin man, in a white sports shirt and black trousers, his hair ruffled, joined the crowd that was now being held back by a guard.

It said much for the muscles and authority of the guards that the panic was quickly controlled. Every window was opened and the dense smoke slowly dispersed.

Scooner, using a bull-horn, kept shouting, "There is no fire. This is a hoax! Everyone is to remain still!"

Like sheep, the crowd obeyed.

Trumbler came up to Scooner.

"Look!" He showed Scooner a plastic container. "A sophisticated smoke bomb, and read . . ."

Scooner read the label stuck on the bomb:

TO HELL WITH RUSSIA! The Anti-Soviet League.

"The sonofabitch is still here," Scooner snarled. "We'll find him!"

A squat KGB man came up.

"No one to leave until we have checked for damage!" he barked.

"Sure," Scooner said. "This is a hoax. I'll talk to these people."

Using his bull-horn, Scooner, now sweating and knowing he was in trouble, explained to the crowd that some joker had let off a smoke bomb and before anyone could leave, names and addresses were needed. Would they all queue up in the lobby and when it had been ascertained that no damage had been done, they would be free to leave.

Relaxing, the crowd began to laugh. They seemed to think it was a good joke against the Soviet Union.

As soon as the first floor had been cleared, the KGB men went through the exhibits, looking for damage. To Scooner's startled surprise, they all seemed to be art experts. One of them going to the icon in its glass case, stared at it, then stepped over the guard rope and found the glass case unlocked.

Watching him, Scooner's heart sank. An alarm should have sounded as the KGB man opened the case.

The KGB man snatched the icon from the case, glared at it, then turned to Scooner, his face purple with rage.

"This is a fake!" he screamed.

Hearing this, Trumbler turned and rushed to the nearest telephone.

A black 280SL Mercedes pulled into a disused builder's yard and into a shed out of sight of the street.

Ed Haddon consulted his watch. Give or take, he had a ten-minute wait. He was completely relaxed. His confidence in Lu Bradey was unshakeable. The operation had been well planned. Only bad luck could turn it sour, and Haddon didn't believe in either bad or good luck.

Nine minutes later, an ambulance drove into the yard. A tall black man slid out, ran to the double gates and closed them. The driver ran over to Haddon and gave him the thumbs-up sign.

"No problems, boss," he said, beaming. "Sweet as honey."

The tall black had opened the rear of the ambulance and the Vietnamese girl, no longer looking pregnant, wearing dark red slacks and a yellow blouse, clothes that had been waiting for her in the ambulance, came running over to Haddon. She thrust the icon through the window. Haddon examined it, satisfied himself it was the original, then produced three envelopes. He gave two of them to the blacks, and the third to the Vietnamese girl.

"Okay," he said. "Get the gates open and get lost."

The tall black opened the gates, and with a wave of his hand, Haddon drove just below the legal speed limit, out on to the street and headed for the airport.

Arriving at the airport parking lot, he reached for a suitcase, lying on the back seats. Opening it, pushing aside his overnight articles, he pressed a concealed spring and the false bottom of the case opened. He slid in the icon, then snapped the suitcase shut and leaving the Mercedes, walked over to the departure centre. He checked in under a false name. The girl recognising an executive big-shot gave him a sexy smile.

"The Miami flight in ten minutes," she said.

Nodding, Haddon paused to buy a copy of *Time*, then proceeded to the departure lounge, joining other businessmen, also on their way to Miami.

Arriving at Miami airport, he hired a Lincoln from the Hertz desk and headed for Paradise City. As he edged his way into the traffic, he glanced at his watch. The time was 15.05. Nice going, he thought. Not for a moment did he wonder what was happening to Lu Bradey, but he smiled, imagining the commotion that must be going on at the Fine Arts museum. Bradey most certainly would have taken care of himself, and was probably now heading for New York.

An hour later, Haddon walked into Kendrick's Gallery where Louis de Marney was nervously moving around, shifting objects, putting them back in their original places, tense with waiting. At the sight of Haddon, he caught his breath.

"Claude?" Haddon said curtly.

"In his office . . . waiting," Louis said. "Did—did you get it?"

"What do you think?"

Haddon walked through the gallery, then pushed open Kendrick's door. Kendrick was pacing up and down, his wig askew.

"Ed! Chéri!" he exclaimed. "I've been in utter torment! Have you . . . ?"

Haddon closed the door and walked over to Kendrick's desk. He laid the suitcase on the desk, snapped open the locks, pressed the spring, and turning with a wide smile, handed the icon to Kendrick.

"Dear God!" Kendrick muttered. "And how I worried! I should have known! Marvellous, marvellous man!" Then he stared apprehensively at Haddon. "Any trouble? No horrid violence?"

Haddon's smile widened.

"Went as sweet as honey. Now it's your turn to do some work."

"Yes . . . yes." Kendrick lumbered to the door and called for Louis. Then he went to his desk telephone and dialled his cousin's number. When Maverick answered, Kendrick said, "The goods have arrived. I am sending Louis to you right away." He listened, then said, "A beautiful job. No problems," and he hung up.

Louis slid into the room. At the sight of the icon, his little eyes lit up.

"My pet," Kendrick said. "Wrap this, and take it to Roger. He is waiting and ready. You know what to do."

Louis picked up the icon and studied it.

"I think my colours are nicer, don't you, baby?"

"Hurry . . . hurry."

When Louis had gone, Kendrick went to the liquor cabinet.

"I am in such a nervous state, I must have a brandy," he said. "Dear Ed. Join me."

"No, thanks. Nervous? I told you I'd get it, and I've got it. The time to get nervous is when the real heat is on which will be around two hours time."

"Yes. I can imagine. Those Vietnamese? The police will be horrid to them."

"So what? They know nothing. The only two in on this are the pregnant girls. The one with the smoke bomb got rid of her belly basket in a toilet. Her clothes were reversible. She has false papers. She left the toilet and mingled with the crowd: just another art lover. Even if the cops catch up with her, she won't talk. The girl who gave me the icon is probably in New York by now, and lost."

Kendrick lifted his wig to mop his bald head.

"And Lu?"

Haddon laughed.

"Lu is the one man you never need worry about."

Kendrick sipped his brandy, then came to his desk and sat down.

"So, it now remains for that dreadful Lepski to carry the icon to Switzerland, then we are rich."

"That's it," Haddon said. "It's a sweet operation." Then he paused and stared at Kendrick. "Always provided your buyer doesn't stall at the last moment. Six million is a lot of loot to find. Are you sure of him, Claude?"

"Certainly. He is enormously rich. Yes, I am sure of him." Claude again sipped his brandy, then an uneasy thought crept into his mind. Could he be sure when dealing with Herman Radnitz? Could anyone be sure when dealing with this ruthless tycoon?

Even another gulp of brandy didn't soothe his jumping nerves.

Fred Scooner was trying to placate Karrass Keremski, Head of the KGB security guards.

"For God's sake, take it easy," he was saying. "Okay, the icon has been stolen, but it *must* still be in the building. The moment the smoke started, I had all exits sealed. No one has left the museum. The thief is still here, and the icon is still here. This is a stunt by the Anti-Soviet League to cause trouble. Everyone will be checked, and their names and addresses taken. Ten of my men are already searching the whole museum. It's my bet, they'll find the icon."

Keremski glowered.

"The icon is gone!"

Scooner turned away. He went to the head of the steps and looked down at the patient queue, giving their names and addresses, and submitting to a body search.

Hurley, guarding the exit doors, let them out as he or she handed him a clearance chit. The operation was going smoothly, and Scooner was satisfied that no one could smuggle out the icon.

Lu Bradey, in his white sports shirt and black trousers laid a false English passport before one of the security checkers.

"I'm staying at the Delaware hotel," he said. "I will be sight-seeing all day, and then I go on to Ottawa: Hotel Central."

The guard surveyed him: just another goddamn tourist, he thought, nodded and passed over the clearance chit. Bradey submitted to the body search, then walked out, hailing a taxi that drove him to the Delaware hotel.

Within an hour and a half, with some thirty guards working fast, the last visitors had gone.

Scooner was relaxing. The icon could not, repeat not, have been smuggled out of the museum. It was now just a matter of careful searching to find it. Then he became aware that one of his men was signalling to him. It was a discreet signal and Scooner's heart sank.

"I'll be right back," he said to Keremski, and walked over to where the guard was standing.

"Something odd here, sir," the guard said. "In one of the women's toilets."

Trumbler joined them.

"What is it?" he asked.

Together he and Scooner entered the toilet and the guard pointed to an egg shaped wicker basket with elastic straps, lying on the floor.

"What in God's name is this?" Scooner muttered.

"Don't touch it!" Trumbler said sharply. He moved forward, crouched and examined the basket, then he looked up

70

at Scooner. "That's how the smoke bomb was brought in. Those Vietnamese! Two of them were pregnant!"

"Sir."

Scooner turned to find another guard at his side.

"In the gent's loo on the second floor, there is a disguise."

"Hell!" Scooner exclaimed. "You stay here," he went on to the first guard, then following the second guard, followed by Trumbler, he walked up the steps to the second floor. The guard opened the door of one of the men's toilets and stood aside. On the floor was a black coat, a bald wig, a heavily padded waistcoat and a clerical collar.

Trumbler immediately read the photo.

"That fat clergyman! The Vietnamese!" he exclaimed. Shoving past Scooner, he raced down to the lobby. His inquiry as to whether a fat clergyman had been checked out brought a negative reply.

Scooner joined him.

"Those Vietnamese!"

"I have all their names, sir," one of the guards said. "They are all staying at the Brotherhood of Love hostel."

"When you were checking them out, did you notice two of the women were heavily pregnant?" Scooner demanded.

"I didn't notice, sir, but Hurley might. He took the check-out slips and let them out."

Trumbler said, "I'm calling the Boss," and dived for a telephone.

Scooner crossed to where Chick Hurley was standing by the exit doors. The excitement over, Hurley was again thinking of his wife. He came to attention as Scooner grabbed his arm.

"Did you see two of those Vietnamese women who were pregnant leave?" Scooner demanded.

Hurley blinked at him.

"No, sir. Of course one of them was taken away in an ambulance, but I didn't see the other one."

"Ambulance?" Scooner glared at him. "What ambulance?"

Hurley stiffened.

"Why, the one you sent for, sir."

"I sent for? What the hell are you yammering about?"

71

Sweat began to drip down Hurley's fat face.

"Well, sir, when the smoke started, the clergyman told me this Viet woman, shocked, was in labour, and you had called an ambulance. The ambulance arrived moments later, and two black men with a stretcher carried her out. She was in great pain, sir. As you had ordered the ambulance, I let them out. Did I do wrong?"

Scooner stood motionless, his eyes glazed like a man who had been hit over the head with a length of lead piping.

Trumbler, rushing from the telephone box, grabbed his arm.

"There's no such hostel as the Brotherhood of Love!"

Scooner drew in a deep breath. He now knew the icon had not only been stolen, but had been smuggled out of the museum.

"It's gone, Jack! You take over. I'll talk to this KGB creep. Man! Are we in trouble!"

Trumbler rushed back to the telephone. Thirty minutes later, every exit from the United States of America was slammed shut.

At 11.00 on Wednesday morning, a sleek, impressive-looking van pulled up outside the Lepskis' bungalow. On each side of the van's buff-coloured cabin was the magic word: *MAVERICK*. The van and the name caused curtains to be pulled back, neighbours to walk casually into their gardens and envious eyes to stare.

Carroll had been waiting expectantly, and seeing the van arrive, seeing the commotion it caused was a highlight of her life.

The van driver, a tall, elegant, blond young man, wearing a buff-coloured uniform, laced with brown braid, and a buff-coloured peak cap with a brown visor, carrying a vast parcel, arrived at the Lepskis' front door.

Carroll practically tore the front door off its hinges as she opened up.

Giving Carroll a shy, smirking smile, this beautiful young man insisted on coming in to unpack the parcel.

"Mr Maverick wishes to be absolutely sure that you are completely satisfied, madam."

Carroll was reluctant to let this glamorous young man into her home. The living-room, as usual, was in an utter mess. It took Carroll until late in the afternoon to straighten up. Somehow, she and Lepski always left the living-room in a state of chaos before retiring for the night. How this happened, Carroll never understood, but happen it did.

But the blond van driver was so charming, so apparently oblivious to the mess, she regained confidence.

The parcel was unpacked.

"The suitcase with your initials, madam, is packed with your dresses, shoes and handbags," the driver said. "Mr Lepski's case is empty. Here is the vanity box. Mr Maverick particularly wants to know if it pleases you."

Carroll was still drooling over the vanity box, long after the van had driven away. Apart from a de luxe assortment of expensive cosmetics, it included a baby mink crocodile wallet for traveller's cheques, her initials embossed in gold, as well as a matching sleeve for her passport and a manicure set, so elegant that Carroll was nervous of touching it.

An hour later, three of her best girl friends, unable to contain their curiosity any longer, came knocking on her front door.

This was Carroll's moment of glory. The little bungalow resounded to squeals of envy, admiration and warm delight as she displayed her purchases.

None of her friends were content until she had put on each dress and paraded around the messy living-room. As all her friends also had messy living-rooms, none of them cared a damn about the background.

They feasted their eyes on Maverick's creations, dreaming of the day when someone would leave them money so they too could compete with Carroll.

While Carroll was changing into another creation, her closest friend cut sandwiches, using up the cold chicken and ham that Carroll had put aside for her husband's dinner. They also attacked Lepski's bottle of Cutty Sark which Carroll had

73

replaced. The party became quite a party, even to a glee song, led by Carroll at her most powerful, with the others filling in, in a noise that set the neighbours' dogs howling.

Finally around 18.00, the party broke up. The girls had to rush back to their homes to scrape up something for their husbands to eat. Carroll, a little tight, once again sat before the vanity box to finger the gorgeous bottles and sighing with delight.

Then Lepski arrived.

Lepski had had a trying day. Chief Fred Terrell had returned from his vacation. Lepski had had to fill him in on the various crime happenings since he had been away. Although of little importance, Lepski liked to make out that if he hadn't been in charge, Paradise City would have been on its knees. Terrell, who knew Lepski well, had listened patiently, nodded and puffed at his pipe. He summed up: ten cars stolen: ten cars recovered, three minor break-ins and five drunken drivers.

"Okay, Tom," Terrell said. "Now, you get off and have a good vacation."

Sergeant Beigler came in.

"Report. There's a nut with a rifle, shooting the lights out in a highrise. The squad cars are down there. Should Tom take a look?"

Terrell nodded.

"Okay, Tom, your last job. Take a look."

This was meat and drink to Lepski. He threw himself into his car and belted down Paradise avenue, his siren screaming. He liked nothing better than to make a Rolls, a Bentley, a Caddy swerve out of his way.

Arriving at the scene, he found ten uniformed cops staring up at a distant window of a 17-storey highrise.

"He's up there," one of the cops said. "Shooting."

Lepski patted his gun.

"Let's go," he said.

Aware of a big crowd watching, aware too that a TV crew had arrived, Lepski took his time, walking slowly and purposely towards the entrance to the highrise, hoping the TV creeps were filming him.

74

With three cops and a shivering, elderly janitor, Lepski rode up to the 11th floor.

"That's the door to his apartment, sir," the janitor said as they stepped out into the corridor. "It's Mr Lewishon. I reckon he has bats in his attic."

Lepski, gun in hand, waved the three cops into position, then raising his foot, he slammed it against the lock of the door and the door flew open.

It came as an anti-climax as they rushed into a well furnished room where a fat, elderly man was sitting before an open window with a .22 rifle in his hands.

"Hold it!" Lepski bawled in his cop voice, his gun pointing at the elderly man.

"Ah! The police! How right!" The man laid down his rifle. "Come in. Come in. Look at this disgrace! In broad daylight, people over there have their lights on. It is an utter disgrace! Our good President is continually asking us to save energy, but no one heeds. Lights! Lights! Everywhere are lights!"

When Lepski turned in his report, Beigler and Jacoby laughed themselves sick.

"Okay, you two jerks," Lepski shouted. "I'll be on TV, so laugh that off!"

It so happened, after inquiring, Lepski was told by the Paradise City TV people that the shot of him walking to the highrise had been blacked out by a kid who thought it smart to put his grimy little hand before the lens of the TV camera.

In a sour mood, Lepski, pounding into his bungalow like a fire engine on emergency, bawled, "I'm home! What's for dinner?"

Carroll had just replaced an elegant scent spray in her vanity box. The sound of Lepski's voice jarred her from the dream of how millionaires' wives live down to the sordid reality of how a First Grade detective's wife lives.

"Hi, baby!" Lepski bawled, rushing into the living-room. "What's for dinner? I'm starving!"

Carroll closed her eyes. Her dream evaporated. Back into the reality of life, she stood up.

"Tom! Look at our luggage. Look! There's a suitcase with your initials. Isn't it marvellous?"

Lepski gaped at the suitcases.

"For me? What the hell do I want with a new suitcase? I've already got a suitcase!"

"Your grandfather owned it," Carroll said coldly.

"What's wrong with my grandfather?" Lepski demanded aggressively.

"This is the suitcase you are going away with!" Carroll said slowly and firmly.

Lepski approached the suitcase and examined it. He sucked in his breath.

"Jesus! This must have cost a bomb! Have you gone spending crazy, honey?"

"Look at this!" Carroll pointed to the vanity box.

Lepski stared.

"You bought this?"

"Mr Maverick *gave* it to me."

Lepski peered at the contents of the box. He picked out a perfume spray and squirted his face.

Carroll snatched the spray from him.

"Hmmm . . . sexy," Lepski said. "You mean he gave it to you."

"Yes, and the two suitcases were only a hundred dollars."

"Man! You must have sexed that fag into a real man," Lepski said and grinned. "Trust my baby. What's for dinner?"

"Lepski, can't you really think of anything else but food?" Carroll demanded as she made her way to the kitchen.

"We've gone over all that before," Lepski said, following her. "Let's eat."

As Carroll looked into the refrigerator and realised where those succulent chicken and ham sandwiches had come from, she released a wail of despair.

Lepski, recognising the sound, released an expletive that made Carroll's ears burn.

The news of the audacious theft of the Catherine the Great icon hit the TV news screens at 18.00. The telecaster said that already the President of the United States had talked to the Premier of the Soviet Union. He had assured the Premier that the icon would be recovered. He was offering a $200,000 reward that would lead to its recovery. The Premier of the Soviet Union had ordered the exhibits at the Fine Arts museum to be packed and returned to the Soviet Union immediately under close guard.

The President had told the Premier that all exits had been shut and there was no way the icon could be smuggled out of the country. It was now only a matter of time before the icon was found.

All security forces, the Army and the Navy had been called in for the hunt. The thieves would be found and punished.

It wasn't reported what the Premier had replied.

Kendrick, with Louis, listened to the broadcast and exchanged uneasy glances.

Ed Haddon listened in his suite at the Spanish Bay hotel and grinned.

Lu Bradey, in New York, also listened and also grinned. Even if one of the Vietnamese was tempted by the reward, he had completely covered his tracks. Whatever the possible Vietnamese said, it would only confuse the issue.

Bradey nodded to himself. He felt confident that with the help of First Grade Detective Tom Lepski, the icon would arrive in Switzerland.

five

It was unfortunate that the Miami-Paris flight was scheduled to leave at 18.00. This meant that Lepski had all the morning and afternoon in which to fidget. Soon after 08.00, he began to prowl around the small bungalow while Carroll remained in bed, reading the morning's newspaper.

Having made coffee, Lepski, finding it unrewarding to fidget on his own, entered the bedroom.

"Honey, have you the flight tickets?"

Carroll sighed.

"I have everything. For heaven's sake, go for a walk! I'm taking a bath, then I'm going to the hairdressers. I won't be back until three o'clock."

"What's for lunch?" Lepski asked anxiously.

"Go buy yourself a cheeseburger or something. The kitchen's closed for the vacation."

Lepski moaned softly, then asked, "Have you packed everything?"

"Lepski! Go away!" Then as Lepski moved reluctantly to the door, she asked, "Have *you* packed everything?"

Lepski gaped at her.

"I thought you were doing the packing."

"I've done *my* packing. I am certainly not doing yours! Now, take the paper and leave me to dress. When I have gone, you can pack. Read about this icon that's been stolen.

79

There's a two hundred thousand dollars reward for its recovery."

"Icon? What the hell's an icon?"

"Go away and read!"

Muttering to himself, Lepski went into the living room, sat down and read the two-page spread about the theft of the icon. He was impressed. Every cop in the country was on the alert. The Army and the Navy had been called in. The President was livid with rage and heads were already beginning to roll. What impressed Lepski more than anything was the big reward offered to anyone giving information that would lead to the recovery of the icon.

Lepski became all-cop. This art treasure couldn't come on the open market. It would be bought in secret by some kinky collector. His sharp mind immediately thought of Claude Kendrick. Lepski was sure, but had no proof, that Kendrick dealt in stolen art treasures. This icon was just up Kendrick's crooked alley.

Jumping to his feet, he snatched up the telephone receiver and dialled police headquarters. He bawled to be put through to Beigler.

The cop handling the switchboard, recognised Lepski's voice.

"Joe's busy," he said. "We're right up to our eyes in this crap about the stolen icon. What do you want?"

"If you don't put me through to Joe right this second, I'll have your goddamn guts for garters!" Lepski snarled.

"Okay, okay." There was a long pause, then Beigler came on the line.

"For God's sake, Tom, you're on vacation," he said. "What is it?"

"This icon! Are the cops included in the reward?"

"How would I know? The Big-shot said *anyone*. Maybe cops aren't anyone. What's biting you?"

"That fat fag Kendrick! If anyone's got that icon, he has!"

"Yeah, yeah. Look, Tom, go enjoy your vacation. The Chief thought of Kendrick as soon as the news broke. We have three of our men, plus the FBI, plus the CIA, plus a search warrant going over Kendrick's gallery right now. Just relax and enjoy your vacation," and Beigler hung up.

Lepski released a snort that would have brought a fighting bull to a standstill.

Carroll, dressed, swept in.

"What was that disgusting noise?"

"Nothing . . . nothing."

"Now go and pack. I'll see you around three. 'Bye for now," and Carroll left.

Lepski spent a miserable morning, cramming his new clothes into his new suitcase, wandering around the bungalow, looking constantly at his watch, then driven by hunger, he drove down to a bar, popular with the cops, where he munched a hamburger and drank a beer.

As he was wondering if he should treat himself to another beer, Max Jacoby came in and climbed on a stool at his side. He ordered a cheeseburger.

"Man! This goddamn icon is as lethal as an atomic bomb!" Jacoby said. "The whole coastline has been sealed off. The heat is really something. The Navy is patrolling. The Army won't let any motor cruiser or yacht out. Owners are blocking our lines with complaints."

"How about Kendrick?"

"He's clean. We really turned his gallery over."

Lepski shrugged.

"Okay. So it could be anywhere."

"You can say that again, but with the President this mad, the heat's fierce." Jacoby sighed. "Man! Are you lucky to be on vacation."

"That reward? Suppose you found the icon, think you would collect?"

Jacoby laughed.

"I'm not going to find it, Tom, but even if I did, cops don't get rewards. You told me that once, didn't you?"

"Yeah, but still . . ."

Jacoby finished his cheeseburger, patted Lepski's arm and slid off his stool.

"Back to the grindstone. Have a good vacation."

Lepski returned home. He kept thinking of the two hundred thousand dollar reward. Some creep would eventually squeal and the icon would be found and the creep would collect.

81

He was piling up the ash tray with cigarette butts when Carroll arrived home. He scarcely recognized his wife: she looked so glamorous.

"Pheeeew!" His whistle could be heard at the end of the street. "Baby! You look gorgeous!" And he started to his feet.

Seeing the look in his eyes, Carroll hurriedly backed away.

"Don't you dare come near me! Have you packed?"

Lepski sighed.

"Oh, sure."

"Then what are you doing wearing that ghastly working suit?" Carroll demanded. "You are *not* travelling in that abortion, and what are you thinking of, wearing your hat indoors?"

"Look, baby, I've packed all the new, goddamn clothes."

"Then unpack them! You are travelling in the sports jacket and the dark blue slacks. You are wearing the pale blue shirt and the wine-coloured tie!"

By 17.00, Carroll was also getting fidgety. She kept looking at herself in the lobby mirror, looking at her watch while Lepski, now attired in his new finery, was walking around the living room, humming under his breath.

"Time's getting on," Carroll said. "I hope the taxi won't be late."

"Taxis are never late." Then Lepski gave her a double-take. "Taxi?"

"Are you telling me you haven't ordered a taxi?" Carroll screamed.

Lepski rushed to the telephone. Joe Dukas, who ran the local taxi service and was a good friend of Lepski, told him there was no problem. A taxi would arrive in good time to get them to the airport at 18.00. Smiling smugly, Lepski hung up.

"You know, baby, there are times when you get nervous," he said. "The cab's on its way."

"I can't understand why you are such a good cop," Carroll sighed. "You seem to be a perfect idiot in the smaller things of life." Then she smiled at him. "But I love you, Tom."

Lepski pointed like a gun dog.

"The taxi will take half an hour, so suppose . . ."

"Lepski! You should be ashamed of yourself!"

At 17.15, the taxi arrived and a big, smiling black man came up the path.

"Here we go!" Carroll cried excitedly. "Give him the luggage, Tom."

Lepski handed over the two blue suitcases which the black carried down the path. Lepski was aware that all their neighbours had come out into their gardens. A little boy had a Japanese flag which he was waving. Lepski always referred to him as *Denis the Menace*, but right now the kid seemed full of good-will and cheer.

Carrying the vanity box, Carroll moved on to the path, feeling like a movie star in her glamorous outfit. Then she paused.

"Tom! Did you turn off the electricity and the water?"

Lepski closed his eyes and released a soft moan.

"Just going to do it!"

He rushed back into the bungalow, watched by the neighbours.

Carroll waited, her smile fixed, her foot tapping, aware of the hum of voices as the news was passed on, over the garden fences, that Lepski had forgotten to turn off the electricity and the water. The know-alls wagged their heads with disapproval.

Sudden violent expletives came from the bungalow. Carroll, horrified by the language, ran into the bungalow to find Lepski nursing a bleeding hand.

"The goddamn, sonofabitch tap won't turn!" he bawled. "I'm wounded!"

"The tap is already turned off!" Carroll screamed.

"Okay, so the bastard is off, but I'm bleeding!"

Carroll rushed into the bathroom, found a band-aid and slapped it on Lepski's scratch.

"We're going to miss the plane!"

Slamming and locking the front door, they bolted down the path and piled into the taxi.

The neighbours clapped and cheered.

"Get moving!" Lepski bawled. "We'll miss our flight!"

The black cabby turned in his seat and gave a big friendly smile.

"Take it easy, boss. There's a three-hour hold-up at the airport. You sure have plenty of time."

The little boy with the Japanese flag came running up and, pursing his lips, blew them the loudest raspberry Lepski had ever heard.

Ed Haddon sat in one of the air traffic controller's glass cubicles and looked down at the departure lounge that was crammed with irate passengers.

The air traffic controller knew Haddon was a close friend of his father who was serving a five-year stretch for robbery. He also knew that Haddon was pulling strings to get his father paroled. So when Haddon told him he wanted to see one of his friends get off to Paris without having to mix with the mob, he was happy to lend him his office. He was too busy in the control tower to wonder who Haddon's friend might be.

Haddon smoked a cigar and watched the long line of passengers slowly passing through the customs' barrier. He noted there were two FBI agents and two plain-clothes detectives with the customs men.

Every piece of luggage was opened and searched. The delay was endless. These passengers were on the New York flight. The Miami-Paris passengers were waiting outside the departure lounge.

Lepski's taxi pulled up, and Lepski and Carroll alighted. As Lepski paid off the taxi, he heard a friendly voice saying, "Hi, Tom."

Turning, he found Harry Jackson, a uniformed cop, grinning at him.

"Heard you were off to Europe," he said. "Big deal! Afraid there's one hell of a delay. It's this icon crap."

Lepski glared at the long queue waiting to enter the departure lounge.

"You'd better get in line, Tom," Jackson went on. "I reckon there's a good three-hour wait."

"Not for me!" Lepski said firmly. "This is my goddamn vacation! I'm not standing in any goddamn line. Get me through to the check-in desks, Harry. Come on! Let's go!"

Carroll said, "Lepski! You can't do such a thing! These

poor people might have been waiting hours."

"Screw them!" Lepski said, and snatching up the two suitcases, he followed Jackson through a side door to the check-in lobby. Her face red when she saw how the waiting passengers were glaring, Carroll followed.

The girl at one of the check-in desks gave Lepski a sexy smile.

"Hi, Tom! I have your seats reserved, but there's a delay. Go into the VIP lounge. I'll tell Nancy to organise drinks. What do you fancy?"

Lepski, who was a well-known character and popular at the airport, gave her his big smile.

"Half a pint of Cutty Sark and half a bottle of champagne, sweetheart," he said. He handed over the two suitcases. "I'll bring you back some perfume from Paris."

The girl giggled, then seeing Carroll glaring at her, lost her smile.

"Have a lovely vacation," she said.

As Lepski steered Carroll to the departure lounge, she demanded, "Who was that?"

"I have my friends," Lepski said with a smug smile. "Good cops always have friends."

The Miami FBI agent came over.

"Hi, Tom! You going on this flight?"

The two men shook hands.

"Next flight: Paris," Lepski said.

"There's a delay, but you may as well go through the customs now. This flight has gone through."

Lepski recognised Hermey Jacobs at the customs counter. He and Hermey shot regularly once a week at the Sharpshooter's Club.

"Hi, Hermey!" he bawled. "I'm off to gay Paree!"

Jacobs' face lit up. It was good to see a friend after handling all the rich creeps who kept moaning about opening their baggage.

Suddenly proud of her husband, Carroll followed Lepski up to the counter. She placed her vanity box on the counter and gave Jacobs a big smile.

"Hi, Hermey! How's Mabs?"

Often Carroll and Mabs Jacobs played tennis together.

85

"Beautiful!" Jacobs said. "You look good enough to eat, Carroll." He looked at the vanity box. "My! My! Big deal, huh?"

Although Haddon had nerves of steel, he was now sitting foward, staring down at this scene, and his cigar had gone out.

"Hey!" Lepski plucked at Jacobs' arm, pulling him close. He whispered, "She's got ten ounces of heroin in her panties. Want to take a look?"

Jacobs gave a bellow of laughter, punched Lepski lightly on his chest, then waved them through.

"Watch him, Carroll," he said. "The French girls could fall for him in that suit."

As they crossed to the VIP lounge, Carroll said, "Let's get this straight, Lepski. No French girls . . . right?"

As Lepski was thinking up a reply, Ned Jason, Head of the Customs office, spotted them.

"Why, Tom! Haven't seen you in weeks." He shook hands, then turning to Carroll. "Honey, you look marvellous. You two off to Paris?"

"Yep. The first vacation we've had abroad. This is a hell of a mess, Ned. All this goddamn delay."

"It's this icon thing. The delay is all along the line. Interpol has moved in. You'll have another long delay at Paris."

Jason owed Lepski a favour. A year ago, Jason's son got involved with a whore who tried blackmail. Lepski had fixed her.

"Can you fix something for us, Ned?" Lepski asked. "You draw a lot of water."

The two men looked at each other, then Jason nodded.

"Sure, leave it to me. I'll telex Charles de Gaulle to give you the VIP treatment. You'll be at the head of the queue, and if you show your shield, they'll pass you through pronto. How's that?"

"Fine, and thanks."

They shook hands and Jason hurried away.

"See?" Lepski crowed. "I may be an idiot in little things, but I'm a big deal in my job."

Impressed, Carroll said, "You're marvellous, Tom! I

won't ever let anyone say you are an idiot in little things ever again."

"And don't you say it either." Lepski grinned. "Come on, let's get drunk." He grabbed hold of the vanity box, paused and gaped at her. "For God's sake! What have you in this box . . . lead?"

"If you are too weak to carry it, give it to me!"

Carroll adored the vanity box, but had admitted to herself that it did seem unreasonably heavy.

Watching from the gallery, Haddon slowly relaxed. The vanity box, worth six million dollars, had gone over the first hurdle. Lepski's plane wouldn't arrive now in Paris until 11.00 the following morning. He picked up the telephone receiver and called Lu Bradey at the Sherman hotel, New York.

His talk was brief.

"They'll arrive Paris eleven morning tomorrow," he said. "So far, no problems," and he hung up.

In his turn, Bradey put through a call to Duvine's Paris apartment.

His call was as brief.

"Eleven morning, tomorrow, Charles de Gaulle. No problems," and he hung up.

By the time Carroll and Lepski boarded the Jumbo jet, both of them were in a mellow mood. They had been cosseted by a bright-eyed, pretty hostess who was all over Lepski, and after finishing a second bottle of champagne, Carroll began to like her.

Settled in their seats, with half a bottle of Cutty Sark under his belt, Lepski was inclined to relax and sleep, but his peace was disturbed when, through the window, he saw a small coach arrive and from it spilled some thirty young people. The men and the girls were wearing the modern uniform of Levis and sweat shirts. They came storming into the first class section, shouting to each other in a language Lepski couldn't identify.

He gave Carroll his sour look.

"How these young creeps can afford first class beats me!" he said.

"They have every right to travel as you and me," Carroll said. "Do stop moaning."

Lepski went to sleep.

Carroll woke him when dinner was served. The hostess gave them the VIP treatment. The dinner was excellent. Sitting in the front seats, Lepski was aware of the noise the youngsters were making, but it didn't put him off his food.

After brandy, Lepski stretched out.

"This is the life," he said, patting Carroll's hand, and went to sleep.

After a hearty breakfast, Lepski began to take interest in his surroundings. The hostess told him that they would be arriving over Paris in two hours. She gave him a radio-telegram which read:

Have a ball! Report on the French situation. Expect full details of you-know-what. Joe and the boys.

Carroll, who read over his shoulder, demanded, "What's that mean?"

Lepski, who knew, put on his serious face.

"Just police business, honey."

Carroll eyed him suspiciously.

"Tell that to your grandma," she said. "I know what you-know-what means as well as you do."

Lepski winked at her and patted her hand.

"Just their little joke."

As the plane came in to land at Charles de Gaulle, both Carroll and Lepski stared out of the window. The first glimpse of the Eiffel Tower brought a squeal of excitement from Carroll.

"Oh, Tom! Paris!"

Lepski, staring down at the broad panorama of Paris, bathed in sunshine, felt a surge of excitement he had never experienced before.

As the Jumbo circled the airport and made its run-in, Lepski saw, below, a cluster of people, three TV cameras and crew, some ten press photographers, and three smartly dressed women holding big floral bouquets.

"Jesus!" he exclaimed. "Look at that! Ned must have really turned on the heat for us! Look at our welcome!"

"But it can't be for us!" Carroll said, her eyes sparkling.

"Who else?" Lepski expanded his chest. "I'm telling you, baby, a good cop has good friends. Man! This certainly is the red-carpet treatment."

The hostess came up to them.

"When we land, Mr Lepski, there will be a hostess to take you to the customs," she said.

Lepski beamed at her.

"Thanks, and thanks for a great ride." He turned to Carroll. "See? The big deal!"

As soon as the plane touched down, Lepski, never feeling more important than at this moment, carrying the vanity box and followed by Carroll, was the first passenger to move out on to the platform on the staircase that had been rushed up to the plane's exit.

He looked down at the pressmen, the photographers, the TV crew and their cameras, and at the three smartly dressed women with the bouquets. He beamed and waved, and Carroll, following his example, feeling like the wife of the President, also waved.

Man! Was this a real, goddamn welcome! Lepski thought. Ned Jason had certainly repaid his debt.

Then he felt a sharp tap on his shoulder. Glancing around, he saw a scruffy looking man with a beard, wearing Levis and a sweat shirt, glaring at him.

"Would you kindly move aside, sir," the man said with a thick, foreign accent. "You are holding up the members of the Bolshoi ballet."

Lepski had never heard of the Bolshoi ballet, but Carroll had. She immediately realised the explanation of this welcome and what a horrible gaff they were making. Grabbing hold of Lepski's arm, she practically threw him down the staircase to the tarmac, and dragged him beyond the TV cameras.

Both of them paused to look back.

The scruffy young people were coming from the Jumbo, waving and laughing as the cameras rolled and the three women advanced with their bouquets.

"Idiot!" Carroll hissed. "You should have known!"

A smiling hostess confronted them.

"Mr and Mrs Lepski?" she asked.

"Yeah . . . yeah," Lepski said, deflated.

"Please follow me to the customs. Your baggage will not be delayed."

Well, at least, Lepski thought, as he carried the vanity box with Carroll at his side, Jason had done his best.

Well ahead of the passengers leaving the Jumbo, the Lepskis were conducted to the passport control. As soon as the officer took their passports, he turned to a hard-faced man in plain clothes, muttered something and the man came forward, offering his hand. He gave a speech in French that went right over Lepski's head, but he put on what he hoped would register as an intelligent smile, shook hands and passed towards the customs control.

"Your bags are waiting," the hostess said. "There's no problem, Mr Lepski."

Two customs officials beamed at Lepski, then at Carroll.

"Welcome to Paris, sir," one of them said in English. "Have a good time," and he waved them through.

Lepski grabbed the two suitcases, leaving Carroll to carry the vanity box.

They moved into the arrival lounge which was crowded.

"What do we do now?" Lepski asked, setting down the suitcases.

"We get a taxi," Carroll told him. "I'm going to the ladies room. You get a taxi organised."

"What do you want with the ladies room?" Lepski asked, uneasy to be left on his own.

"Lepski! Get a taxi!" and Carroll walked away.

Lepski blew out his cheeks. He looked around. Where the hell did one get a taxi? Seeing a fat, elderly man waiting, he went up to him.

"Where's the taxi stand, pal?" he asked.

The fat man stared at him.

"I don't understand English," he said in French and walked away.

Lepski made a growling noise, and looked around helplessly. Didn't any of these finks speak English?

A man in uniform walked near him. Lepski grabbed his arm.

"A taxi, pal. Where the hell do I find a taxi?"

The man jerked his thumb in an easterly direction, and walked away.

Lepski decided it would be safer to stay where he was. Carroll would eventually join him.

Muttering to himself, he waited.

Pierre and Claudette Duvine had been at the arrival centre since 10.30. When Lu Bradey's call had come through, they had been in bed. They had been experimenting with a new sexual technique which they both had decided was not worth the energy. Pierre was a great reader of American paperbacks and was always looking for new ideas to give Claudette pleasure. He had released her in an undignified position, to pick up the telephone receiver.

He listened to Bradey's curt message, then rolled off the bed.

"Business, sugar. Charles de Gaulle at eleven."

Claudette moaned.

They were now standing in the arrival centre, watching for the Lepskis. Pierre had hired a Mercedes 280 SL which he had parked in the Charles de Gaulle parking lot. After standing and waiting for some forty minutes, Pierre suddenly nudged Claudette.

"There they are," he said. "Get going."

He had seen Carroll walk away to the ladies room, carrying the vanity box. The box was unmistakable from Bradey's description.

Claudette went into action. She walked to where Lepski was standing, began to pass him, then lurched against him as if she had slipped.

Lepski, always quick on the reflex, caught hold of her, and found himself looking at the most sexy woman he had ever seen. Claudette's sea-green eyes regarded him with a merry twinkle.

"Excuse me," she said, speaking perfect English. "I always fall over handsome men."

Gay Paree! Lepski thought. Man! Have I arrived!

"That's fine with me, beautiful," he said. "I'd do the same in your place."

Claudette laughed. She had a rich, mellow laugh that she

91

had cultivated, knowing few men could resist it.

"Have you just arrived?"

"Yeah. My wife's just gone off to the loo. I'm looking for a taxi."

"That's no worry. I'm Claudette Duvine. My husband is somewhere." Claudette flickered her long, false eyelashes at Lepski.

"Tom Lepski. Where do I get a taxi?"

Then Pierre decided it was time to move into the scene. He came up to Claudette.

"They haven't arrived," he said in English. "I guess they've changed their minds."

"Meet Mr Tom Lepski, Pierre," Claudette said on cue. "This is my husband."

Lepski regarded the handsome, well dressed man and shook hands.

"Mr Lepski has just arrived. He's worried about getting a taxi," Claudette said smiling. "Suppose we give them a lift into Paris?"

"What's the matter with that?" Pierre said. "Where are you staying, Mr Lepski?"

"The Excelsior hotel," Lepski said after hesitating. He had been told over and over again by Carroll the name of the hotel, but he still wasn't sure.

"The Excelsior! That's where we are staying!" Claudette cried. "You must come with us!"

Then Carroll arrived. Introductions were made. For a brief moment, Carroll regarded Claudette suspiciously. She was so chic and sexy, then seeing Pierre, so glamorous, like a movie star, she relaxed.

Both Pierre and Claudette looked at the vanity box Carroll was carrying. Briefly they exchanged triumphant glances. The box Bradey was so worried about, had come through the customs without fuss. Now, they had only to steer it through the Swiss customs.

With Carroll sitting by Pierre's side and Lepski sitting with Claudette in the rear seats, Pierre drove on to the autoroute and headed for Paris.

Both Pierre and Claudette turned on their professional charm. Pierre explained they were on vacation. They lived

92

in Deauville, and were spending a few days in Paris, then they were driving down to the South. Their easy charm smothered the Lepskis like a comforting blanket.

Arriving at the Excelsior hotel, Pierre took the burden off Lepski's shoulders, booking them in, filling up the police card for him, seeing them to their room and tipping the luggage porter while Lepski was wondering what to give him.

"Now you two dears must be exhausted," Claudette said, "Why not take a nap? Look, suppose we get together around eight tonight?" She smiled at Carroll. "Unless you have something else to do. We would so love to show you Paris at night as this is your first visit. Be our guests!"

"We would love that," Carroll said. "How nice of you!"

"Then let's meet in the lobby at eight."

"Aren't they darlings?" Carroll said when they were alone. "Oh, Tom! We are lucky to meet such lovely people."

"He's pretty smooth," Lepski said. "Does this happen to everyone coming to Paris?"

"Oh, Tom! Can't you drop your dreary cop attitude? French men are smooth. Remember Maurice Chevalier?"

"You remember him," Lepski said, eyeing the double bed. "Let's sleep," and he began to undress.

Carroll went to the big window and drew aside the curtain. She looked down at the avenue des Champs-Elysées with its teeming traffic, the Arc de Triomphe, the crowded cafés and the people wandering in the sunshine. She drew in a long breath.

Paris!

All she had dreamed it would be like!

She turned and found Lepski on the bed, beckoning. She unzipped her dress, let it fall to the floor, then threw herself on him.

"Oh, Tom! This is going to be the most marvellous time of our lives!" she exclaimed as Lepski flipped off her bra and slipped off her panties.

After an excellent dinner of lobsters for which Pierre insisted on paying at a small restaurant near the Pont d'Alma, he then insisted they should take a *Bateau-Mouche* and see Paris from the Seine. They boarded the boat, and getting good seats they relaxed, wonder-eyed at the beauty of the bridges, the Louvre, the Conciergerie and the flood-lit Notre Dame.

It was during the return journey that Lepski casually asked Pierre what line of business he was in. Lepski, with his cop training, was always interested in how the other man made a living.

"Antiques," Pierre said. He did have, as a cover, an antique shop in Deauville, run by two elderly and expert sisters. "I'm what is called an art broker, giving advice to people looking for the good stuff. It pays off."

"Antiques, huh? How about this stolen Russian icon?" Lepski asked. "Do you think it could be sold?"

Pierre shook his head.

"Most unlikely. It's too well known. Of course, there are secret collectors, but I think it would be too hot even for them. I understand it is causing some excitement in the States."

Lepski laughed.

"You can say that again. The President's flipping his lid. There's a two hundred thousand dollar reward for its recovery. As soon as the theft was discovered all exits from the States were sealed. Every cop and Fed are searching for it. I'm glad I'm on vacation."

Pierre felt Claudette's shoe touch his leg lightly. She and Carroll were sitting behind the two men.

"Pierre, why don't we take Carroll and Tom to the Crazy Horse?" Claudette asked.

Reacting immediately to her signal, Pierre explained that the Crazy Horse was the best strip-tease in town, and Lepski reacted to this like a bull to a matador's cape.

The show at the Crazy Horse was everything that Pierre had promised, and the girls were gorgeous. Carroll decided that this was Lepski's vacation as well as hers, so she let him enjoy himself, only patting his arm warningly when his whistle made heads turn and the girls on the stage giggle.

Around 02.00, the four wandered back to their hotel. It was agreed that they would all meet for a simple lunch, and the girls would go shopping. Pierre, with a sly wink at Lepski, said they would take a drive through the Bois. This Lepski took as a promise of more interesting diversions than driving around the Bois.

In their bedroom, Pierre and Claudette regarded each other.

"Something bothering you, sugar?" Pierre asked. "That signal you gave me on the boat."

Claudette kicked off her shoes, then flopped on the bed.

"The Russian icon you were talking about with Tom. Tell me more."

Pierre sat down and lit a cigarette.

"It's believed to be the oldest icon known, worth millions. It was brilliantly stolen from the Fine Arts museum in Washington some three days ago. The reaction was fast. As Lepski said there's no way of getting it to Europe. Some secret collector just might buy it."

"Suppose you got it, could you sell it?"

Pierre stared at her.

"What's going on in that smart mind of yours?"

"Could you find a market for it?"

"It's not in our league, sugar. Of course, there's always a market for a unique treasure like that, but I haven't the contacts who could find at least four million dollars. Anyway, I haven't got it."

"You said it was brilliantly stolen."

"It was: a steal of a lifetime."

Claudette raised herself on her elbows and looked at Pierre.

"Who could have organized a steal like that, my treasure?"

For a long moment, Pierre remained still, then his eyes lit up.

"You marvellous darling! Of course! Ed Haddon! Who else?" He jumped to his feet. "Bradey! The vanity box! My God! I'm willing to bet the icon is right here in this hotel!"

Claudette laughed.

"That's my bet too, my treasure."

Pierre began to pace around the room, thumping his fist into the palm of his hand.

"What a beautiful idea! To con a cop to smuggle it out! Haddon! He's brilliant! Sugar! You're the cleverest of the clever!"

"Lu wants us to see the vanity box through the Swiss customs. That must mean he has a client in Switzerland. Who?"

"Wait." Pierre sat down, crushed out his cigarette and lit another.

Claudette flopped back on the bed, closed her eyes and waited.

Finally, Pierre said, "The only man I know of who lives in Switzerland and who has the right money is Herman Radnitz. He could be the client."

Claudette opened her eyes.

"Isn't he the horrible man you once sold a picture to?"

"That's the man."

"Suppose we had the icon, could you do a deal with him?"

Pierre hesitated.

"Maybe. I do know he's interested in Russian art. If he is Haddon's client, it depends how much Haddon is asking. At a guess, eight million. If Radnitz was offered the icon for five million . . ."

Claudette got to her feet, unzipped her dress and carefully folded it.

"We are to switch boxes, aren't we? Lu is only paying us a mean twenty thousand Swiss francs and expenses. He and Haddon will make millions. Switched, we have the icon." She looked at Pierre. "We could live in luxury on money like that for years and years."

"Don't get too excited about this, sugar. We must think of the consequences. We would be double-crossing Lu and Haddon. We would never get any more of their business."

"Would that matter if we had five million dollars?"

"You have a point, but we don't know the icon is in the box nor do we know that Radnitz is the client."

"Think, my treasure. I will take a shower. Let's sleep on it. We have plenty of time."

When she had gone into the bathroom, Pierre's mind became busy.

Just suppose, he thought, that the icon really was in Carroll Lepski's vanity box. What could either Lu or Haddon do to him if he did double-cross them? They couldn't squeal to the cops without getting into trouble themselves. They were no

96

thugs. They wouldn't attempt a Mafia-like revenge. No, there was nothing they could do except accept the inevitable.

Then Pierre's shrewd mind turned to Radnitz. Just suppose Haddon had done a deal with Radnitz. Pierre couldn't think of any other collector with Russian art interests, who had a residence in Switzerland and millions to spend. It must be Radnitz.

This man was dangerous. Pierre had heard rumours that Radnitz had once employed a professional killer. He would have to be very careful how he handled Radnitz.

Five million dollars!

A sum as big as that was worth any risk!

First, he must be sure the icon was in the vanity box. At the first opportunity he must examine the box. If satisfied the icon was in the box, then he must contact Radnitz who would surely do a deal if the price was right.

Even when Claudette took him lovingly in her arms, Pierre couldn't sleep.

The thought of owning five million dollars, to be free forever from debt, made sleep impossible.

He was still awake when the sound of the telephone bell brought him upright. He looked at his watch. The time was 03.30.

"A call for you, sir," the operator told him. "New York calling."

Claudette came awake and switched on the bedside lamp.

"Pierre? This is Lu."

"Hello there, Lu," Pierre said. "I was meaning to call you."

"Well, you didn't, so I am calling you!" There was a rasp in Bradey's voice. "What's the news?"

"No problems." Pierre was cautious, knowing they were speaking on an open line. "Our friends are real friends now. No problems."

"Why haven't you called before?" There was a snarl now in Bradey's voice. "Sure about the problems?"

"I'm sure."

"Right," and the line went dead.

"That was Lu," Pierre said, replacing the receiver. "He seems anxious. Sugar, I think your guess is right."

Claudette snuggled against him.

"I *know* it is right." Her arms slipped around him. "Show me how a millionaire makes love."

Pierre showed her.

six

Carrying an over-night case and a gift-wrapped parcel, Ed
Haddon took a cab from Kennedy airport to the Sheraton
hotel where he found Lu Bradey in the main bar, nursing a
Scotch on the rocks.

For a change, Bradey was as himself, wearing a dark
lounge suit, his hair in a crew cut, his thin features pallid,
his dark eyes alert. He lifted a hand, and Haddon joined him.
Bradey signalled to a waiter. Haddon said he would have a
Bourbon straight.

"Any news?" he asked as he lit a cigar.

"I talked to Duvine not an hour ago. No problems," Bradey
said. "He must be handling the job beautifully. He says the
Lepskis are now old friends. No problem with the French
customs."

The waiter brought Haddon's drink. When he had gone,
Haddon sipped, then said, "Good news. Now the Swiss customs."

"Pierre will drive them to Monaco, then to Montreux.
He'll pick one of the small Swiss customs posts. He knows
what he is about."

"Seen the newspapers?" Haddon pulled at his cigar.

"Yeah. Plenty of fuss: plenty of heat."

"Front page news even in the continental papers."

"Well, we expected it."

"Yes." Haddon finished his drink. "I have the replica of the vanity box." He nodded to the gift wrapped parcel by his feet. "You're taking it to Montreux . . . right?"

"To the Montreux Palace hotel when I hand it to Duvine who will switch. Something bothering you, Ed?"

"Could present a problem, Lu. A man carrying a lady's vanity box could attract cop attention."

Bradey chuckled.

"I've thought of that. My girl friend's coming with me."

Haddon eyed him.

"I didn't know you had a girl friend."

"Oh, sure. She's a nice piece of flesh. She's out of her tiny mind at the thought she's going to Switzerland."

"Can you trust her? You know how women will yak. They can't even keep their sex lives to themselves."

"You don't have to worry about Maggie. She's so dumb she thinks Richard Nixon is a pop singer. She does exactly what I tell her to do."

Haddon shrugged.

"Okay. It's a good way to get the box into Switzerland. Now, how about the Duvines?"

Bradey finished his drink.

"What about them?"

"All this goddamn publicity. Every paper in the world is carrying a photo of the icon and a description and what it is worth. On the plane, I got thinking. Would you say the Duvines are smart?"

"Couldn't be smarter. That's why I'm using them."

"Do you think they are that smart they could guess what's in the vanity box?"

Bradey stiffened and a look of alarm jumped into his eyes.

"With all this publicity," Haddon went on, "it struck me if they are really smart, they could guess right. We are paying them only twenty thousand Swiss francs and expenses, and there's a reward of two hundred thousand dollars. You know them. I don't. Think we can trust them not to pull a double-cross?"

Tiny sweat beads appeared on Bradey's forehead.

"I don't know. They're always in debt. Two hundred thousand would be a hell of a temptation." He thought, then

100

shook his head. "No. If they claimed the reward the French police would investigate them and that's something the Duvines couldn't afford. They are in all kinds of rackets. No, I'm sure they wouldn't dare go for the reward."

"Let's take this a step further," Haddon said, "but first let's have another drink."

Bradey signalled the waiter who brought refills.

"Go on," Bradey said uneasily when the waiter had gone.

"They are going to switch boxes. Suppose when they get the Lepski box, they vanish," Haddon said, staring at Bradey. "Have they any big contacts? Someone they could sell the icon to?"

Bradey took out his handkerchief and wiped his forehead.

"I doubt it. The Duvines deal with the little fish. No one who has millions to spend."

"Have you wondered who Kendrick's client is?" Haddon asked.

Bradey nodded.

"Could only be Herman Radnitz . . . right?"

"My thinking too. He fits the scene: Kendrick has had dealings with him. He has a villa in Zurich. He's interested in Russian art, and he has money." Haddon paused, then asked, "Do you know if Duvine has ever had contact with him?"

Bradey thought, and his expression became more and more unhappy.

"Come to think of it, I believe I did hear he sold a painting to Radnitz about a year ago."

"So he could go to Radnitz with the icon, offer it at a cut-throat price and double-cross us?"

Bradey shifted uneasily.

"Well, yes. Duvine would dig up his father's grave if he thought there was money in the coffin."

"And Radnitz would deal with him?"

"That sonofabitch would deal with anyone to save a million."

"My thinking." Haddon sipped his drink. "Looks as if we have a problem, Lu."

"We could be jumping to conclusions. Duvine might not guess the icon is in the box."

"I smell a double-cross," Haddon said quietly. "If Duvine is as smart as you say, he'll have guessed right."

Bradey crossed and recrossed his legs.

"We have time. The Duvines and the Lepskis are now in Paris. They drive to Monte Carlo on 14th. They leave for Montreux on 20th. If Duvine plans to double-cross us, he will wait until Lepski has carried the icon through the Swiss customs. So we have nine days."

Haddon brooded, staring into space while Bradey sat still. He had tremendous faith in Haddon's talent for solving problems.

Finally, Haddon said, "The plan is that Duvine switches the boxes at the Montreux Palace hotel, delivers it to you at the Eden hotel, Zurich, and you pay him twenty thousand Swiss francs and his expenses. Kendrick will already be at the Eden. You give him the box, and he takes it to his client, gets paid and gives us our share. That's the operation as planned. Now, if Duvine plans to double-cross us, when he has switched the boxes, he will drive to Zurich, but not to the Eden hotel. He will go to Radnitz's villa which I understand is some way out of Zurich on the lake. He will make a deal with Radnitz, get paid and vanish."

"This is all surmise," Bradey said, wiping his forehead with his handkerchief. "I've worked with Duvine for years. I find it hard to believe he would double-cross us."

"We are going to assume he *is* going to double-cross us," Haddon said, his face like stone. "When so much money is involved, I trust no one except you. So we are going to assume Duvine will try to pull a smart one and we must take precautions."

"What precautions?"

"We will beat him to the punch. He and his party will arrive at the Montreux Palace hotel on the 20th. You and your girl friend will arrive on the 18th. You will tell the reception clerk that you will be leaving on the 21st, but you want to reserve a room for a friend who is a friend of the Duvines. You want a room on the same floor and near the Duvines' reservation. When Duvine arrives, you will give him the duplicate box and tell him you are leaving for the Eden hotel and you will wait for him to deliver the Lepskis'

102

box. On the 21st, you will leave the hotel, making sure Duvine sees you go. You will stop somewhere close to Montreux, send your girl on to Zurich, put on a disguise and return to the Montreux Palace hotel in the name of the friend you have reserved a room for. From then on, you will not let Duvine out of your sight while he is in the hotel. When he has switched the boxes, you will jump him, take the box, pay him off and drive to the Eden hotel. In this way we forestall a double-cross. What do you think?"

Bradey thought, then finally he nodded.

"The idea is sound, but we mustn't forget, if Duvine is really planning a double-cross, he must already be dreaming of owning at least five million dollars. He could turn rough, and he's bigger than I am. Suppose he bashes me and bolts? If I had his muscles, that's what I would do."

Haddon smiled grimly.

"When you arrive at Geneva, you will buy a gun. I will give you the address of a man who will sell you a gun without asking questions."

Bradey's eyes popped wide.

"No! I've never touched a gun! No violence! That's strictly out, Ed!"

"This operation involves three million dollars: one for you: two for me," Haddon said, a snarl in his voice. "The gun needn't be loaded. If Duvine turns rough, all you have to do is to wave the gun in his face and that'll quiet him down. There must be no slip-up on this, Lu." He took from his wallet a card and wrote an address. "Just mention my name. There will be no problem, but get the gun."

Bradey hesitated, grimaced, then took the card.

"Maybe Duvine isn't going to double-cross us," he said without much hope. "Maybe we are making a mountain out of a molehill."

Haddon picked up the gift-wrapped parcel and placed it on Bradey's knees.

"I'm going to bed. Don't worry about mountains. Don't worry about molehills. Just make sure Kendrick gets the icon and we get our money."

Leaving Bradey staring uneasily at the gift-wrapped parcel, Haddon walked across the bar and towards the elevators.

Vasili Vrenschov was Herman Radnitz's Russian contact. He was a squat, heavily built man with balding head and eyes like black beans set in white dough.

He lived in a modest three-room apartment at Sellinburen, just outside Zurich. This apartment was owned by his Swiss mistress, allowing him to live there without tiresome police interference. He spent much of his time commuting to Moscow, and he was highly thought of by the Soviet upper échelon.

This morning, he had received a telephone call from Radnitz who had invited him to lunch at the Villa Hélios, one of Radnitz's many luxury homes, which was situated a few kilometres outside Zurich, set in two acres of ornamental gardens by the lake with its own harbour and motor boats, to say nothing of a luxury yacht on which Radnitz, when in the mood, entertained.

Vasili Vrenschov was always pleased to receive an invitation from Radnitz. He had arranged a number of lucrative deals with Radnitz and the Kremlin, and Radnitz had always paid him a commission which was credited to Vrenschov's numbered account in the Bank of Zurich: money that the Kremlin knew nothing about.

Leaving his shabby Beetle VW car in the parking bay, Vrenschov mounted the marble steps that led to the impressive portals of the villa. He pressed the door bell and turned to survey the magnificent flower beds and looked enviously at the harbour, the yacht and the view of the lake.

The doors were opened and an elderly butler gave him a little bow.

"Mr Radnitz is expecting you, Mr Vrenschov," he said. "Please follow me."

"Good to see you again, Mythen. Tell me, what have you arranged for my lunch?" Vrenschov asked as he removed his hat and walked into the vast hall, decorated with suits of armour and splendid tapestries.

"Whitstable oysters and Scotch grouse, sir," Mythen said, smiling. He knew what a glutton this Russian was. "The oysters were flown out from England this morning."

Vrenschov rolled his eyes.

"Splendid! And Mr Radnitz? I trust he is well."

"He appears to be in excellent health, sir," Mythen said and led Vrenschov down a long corridor to Radnitz's study.

Radnitz was seated behind a big, antique desk which was littered with papers. As Vrenschov walked in, he rose to his feet with a wide smile of welcome.

"Good to see you, Vasili," he said, coming around the desk to shake hands. "Good of you to come at such short notice. Sit down. A little Vodka?"

Vrenschov settled his bulk in a chair near the desk.

"That would be nice, Mr Radnitz. You are too kind."

Mythen served Vodka in large crystal goblets with crushed ice.

"A cigar?"

"Nothing I would like better."

Mythen took a cigar from a box on the desk, clipped the end, presented it to Vrenschov, offered a light, then with a bow, he left the room.

"Madame? Is she well?" Radnitz asked, sitting behind his desk.

"Yes, thank you. She finds the Zurich climate not to her taste, but she survives."

Radnitz paused to light his cigar, then lifting his glass, nodded to Vrenschov who raised his glass, then drank.

There was a slight pause, then Radnitz said, "I thought it is time we had a talk, Vasili. It is now three months since we last met. Have you any news for me?"

Vrenschov lifted his fat shoulders.

"The Kazan dam?"

Radnitz's hooded eyes hardened.

"What else but the Kazan dam?"

"Yes. Well, you may be sure that I am promoting your interests, Mr Radnitz, as I always do and will."

"And . . . ?"

"This is, of course, an enormous undertaking, Mr Radnitz," Vrenschov said with an oily smile. "The cost . . ."

"We have gone into all that," Radnitz said, a snap in his voice. "I am prepared to finance half the project. Your people the other half. My technicians will assist and advise. That is my proposal. I now want to know what your people are doing about it."

"Well, to be frank, Mr Radnitz," Vrenschov paused to sip his drink. "My people are hesitating. As you can be sure, I have pressed your case, but they think they should consult other contractors to see if the dam can be built for less money."

A tiny flame of rage flickered in Radnitz's eyes and immediately vanished.

"No other contractor can build the dam for less, and certainly not as well as I can."

"I am quite sure that is correct, but my people are difficult. They are investigating further in spite of what I advise. So, there is a delay. I am confident that before very long, matters will be arranged in your favour."

There came a tap on the door and Mythen entered.

"Lunch is served, gentlemen," he announced.

The oysters were succulent and the grouse impeccable, served with a 1959 Margaux, followed by cheese and a champagne sorbet.

While the two men ate, Radnitz talked lightly of this and that, not referring to business, but Vrenschov knew that after lunch he would come under pressure. His past dealings with Radnitz warned him that Radnitz was a ruthless negotiator and he would have to handle him with kid gloves.

Finally, the two men returned to the study, sat down with brandies and cigars, then Radnitz opened fire.

"You and I, Vasili, have had a happy and profitable association," he said, staring with his hooded eyes at Vrenschov. "We have done four deals together. You have been paid, into your numbered account, some ninety thousand Swiss francs as commission which your masters know nothing about."

Vrenschov smiled. He was too old a hand to react to any hint of blackmail. A Swiss numbered account gave complete security.

"My people know nothing about my Swiss account and will know nothing about it, Mr Radnitz," he said.

Radnitz realised this smiling Russian was not blackmail

material. He nodded, and changed tactics.

"If I get the Kazan dam contract through your efforts, Vasili, I think I promised you a quarter of a million Swiss francs."

Vrenschov smiled again.

"That was your kind arrangement, and you may be sure I am doing my very best in your favour, but, as I have said, my people insist on getting other tenders."

Radnitz studied the end of his cigar, his toad-like face expressionless.

"It seems to me," he said finally, "that a lever is needed to bring your masters down on my side."

"A lever? This I don't understand."

"The Catherine the Great icon," Radnitz said, watching Vrenschov closely, but the fat Russian merely lifted his eyebrows.

"Ah, yes," he said. "I hear that it has been stolen when on exhibit in Washington. What can it have to do with the Kazan dam?"

Radnitz controlled his impatience.

"Your masters are making considerable political capital out of the theft. The theft has put the President in a very awkward position. He is not popular. The world press are critical of him. He has taken immediate precautions the icon does not leave the States and by sealing all exits, he is causing considerable inconvenience to the public who are already protesting, blaming the President. From their point of view, I understand this. Very few Americans care a damn about a Russian icon and to have delays and baggage checks at all airports, restrictions on ships and so on makes the President very unpopular."

"That is regrettable," Vrenschov said with a sly smile, "but what has your President's troubles to do with my people?"

"Come Vasili, you know as well as I do, any trouble that affects the President is joyful news at the Kremlin."

Vrenschov laughed: a harsh guttural sound.

"Off the record, Mr Radnitz, I would say you were correct."

"It is said that the President has assured your Premier that the icon is still in the States, and before very long, it will be recovered."

"Yes, this is so. Pravda has published an account of the conversation, but it may take months or even years to find it, if the thief is prepared to wait." Vrenschov passed his brandy glass under his fat nose, sniffing at the aroma. "Is it possible that this exit check, delaying travellers, could continue indefinitely until the icon is found?"

"No. I would imagine the check will continue for at least a month, causing the President more and more trouble, then it will gradually be lifted under the pressure of public complaints."

"That would be the thief's opportunity?"

"No. There would be spot checks, sudden searches. He would have to have very strong nerves to attempt to smuggle the icon abroad."

Vrenschov finished his brandy.

"Happily, Mr Radnitz, this isn't in my province. We seem to have moved away from the Kazan dam which is."

"I was talking about a lever," Radnitz said. "Have some more brandy, my dear Vasili."

"That is kind." Vrenschov helped himself liberally from the cut-glass decanter. "Splendid brandy."

"I take it your masters would be glad to have the icon back?"

"Of course. The icon is one of the finest exhibits in the Hermitage. It always attracts great interest with the tourists, and its value is incalculable."

Radnitz pulled at his cigar.

"This is the lever I have mentioned. Just suppose I was in the position to return the icon to the Hermitage and give you proof that the President has lied that the icon is still in the States would you think your masters would be pleased enough to give me the Kazan dam contract? Just suppose I can prove that the icon left the States the day after it had been stolen in spite of the security precautions, involving all the police, the Federal Bureau of Investigation, the CIA, the Army and the Navy. Well handled, the publicity in the world press, once the story was cleverly leaked, would make the President a laughing stock, would it not?"

108

vrenschov inclined his head.

"Yes. That is obvious, Mr Radnitz. Are you in the position to return the icon or is this just supposition?"

"It depends on your people," Radnitz said. "If I get the Kazan dam contract, they will get the icon."

Vrenschov sucked in his breath.

"Mr Radnitz, I have dealt with you for some time and I have come to rely on any statement you make. Then can I take it you have the icon?"

"I did not say that. I said I could get it. It will cost me money, but I'm prepared to pay for the icon provided I get the contract."

"It is no longer in the States?"

"No."

Vrenschov waited, hoping Radnitz would say where it was, but as Radnitz remained silent, he ventured, "You can guarantee its return?"

"Provided your people guarantee me the dam contract." Radnitz said, looking directly at Vrenschov. "We can make the exchange here. You get the icon. I get the contract."

"This is a very interesting proposal, Mr Radnitz. I will leave for Moscow tomorrow," Vrenschov said. "I can tell my people that the icon has in fact left the States?"

"You can tell them that and they can have it within ten or fifteen days."

Vrenschov nodded.

"You may be sure I will do my very best to promote your interests, Mr Radnitz, but, of course, I can't tell how my people will react. The dam will cost an enormous sum. I hope they will consider the icon enough to tip the scales in your favour."

"That, of course, is up to them." Determined to make some profit from the Russians, Radnitz went on, "Even if they don't give me the contract, I would be willing to buy the icon from my contact if your masters would be willing to pay for it."

"How much would it cost, Mr Radnitz?"

Mindful that it was his intention not to pay Kendrick anything for the icon, Radnitz said, "Six million dollars." Seeing Vrenschov flinch, he added, "On the open market, the icon would be worth at least twenty million dollars. Your masters would not only be getting it cheaply, but would be able to make considerable political capital. Who knows? The President might even re-imburse them. To avoid more unwelcome publicity, it is very possible, he would do this."

"So I have two propositions," Vrenschov said. "Either you get the dam contract and the icon is returned or you don't get the contract, but you will sell the icon to my people for six million dollars. Is that correct?"

Radnitz got to his feet.

"You understand perfectly, my dear Vasili. Get me the contract and I will pay you a quarter of a million Swiss francs. If you fail, but your masters pay six million dollars for the icon, I will pay you fifty thousand Swiss francs. Obviously, it will be to your advantage to press hard for the contract."

"And you can be sure I will, Mr Radnitz."

The two men shook hands.

"You will hear from me within a week," Vrenschov said as Radnitz walked with him to the door.

"Mythen has put a little parcel in your car," Radnitz said. "With the compliments to madame."

"How kind! How thoughtful!" Vrenschov's greedy eyes lit up.

Radnitz smiled, then waved good-bye.

On the third day of their stay in Paris, Pierre Duvine took the Lepskis on a sight-seeing tour. Pierre knew Paris like the back of his hand. After a brief tour of the Louvre, he took them to Notre Dame, then to the Ste Chapelle, and finally to the top of the Eiffel Tower. His commentary was so interesting, even Lepski began to accept this cultural tour.

When they had heard what Pierre proposed, Lepski and Carroll, in their hotel room, had their usual fight.

Lepski said the hell with sight-seeing. He wanted to walk the streets and see the way the French lived. Who needed to look at dreary museums?

Carroll would have none of it.

"It is time, Lepski, for you to have some culture! All you think about is crime, food and women. You are going to take this chance to improve your mind!"

Making a noise like a wasp trapped in a bottle, Lepski submitted.

They returned to the hotel at 17.50, all of them slightly weary and footsore.

"Tonight we go to the Tour d'Argent," Pierre said as they entered the hotel lobby. "One of the great restaurants of Paris. Then we will go to the Lido. I have booked a table." He nudged Lepski. "Georgeous girls."

Lepski immediately brightened.

"Fine. How about a drink, Pierre? Let the girls go up, and you and me rinse our tonsils."

"Lepski! Must you be so vulgar?" Carroll exclaimed.

"You two go on up," Lepski said, and catching hold of Pierre's arm, hurried him towards the bar.

This was the opportunity Claudette had been waiting for. As the two girls walked down the corridor to their rooms, she said, "Carroll, dear, that vanity box you have. I'm so envious! I want to persuade Pierre to buy me one just like yours."

"You haven't even seen the inside," Carroll said, unlocking her bedroom door. "Come in. I'll show it to you. It's marvellous!"

They entered the room. Carroll went to a closet, opened it and took out the vanity box, set it on a table and unlocked it.

"Look! Isn't it super?"

Claudette took her time. She encouraged Carroll to take out all the items, examining them while she gave little gasps of admiration until the box was empty. She then examined the interior, declaiming on the workmanship while Carroll, swelling with pride, watched her.

Claudette then closed the box and lifted it to admire the exterior, noting that there was at least three inches more on the outside than the inside.

"It's perfect!" she exclaimed, "but it is a little heavy."

"Yes, but it's so strong! Tom hates carrying it."

Claudette laughed as she set the box down.

"Well, I wouldn't. I must talk to Pierre."

She watched while Carroll, with loving care, replaced all

111

the items, watched as she locked the box, taking note of the key, then said, "Well, darling, have a rest. We'll all meet in the lobby at eight o'clock. I do hope you have enjoyed your day."

"It's been truly wonderful! I can't thank you both enough!" Carroll said. "You are perfect pets! You utterly spoil us. Now tonight. We insist that you be our guests. You have done so much for us . . . now, please . . ."

"Well, of course." Claudette smiled. "But it is our pleasure. We are so happy to have found such good friends. All right, I will tell Pierre."

Returning to her room, Claudette waited impatiently for Pierre who finally arrived an hour later, looking a little flushed.

"My God!" he exclaimed, holding his head. "How that man can drink! What news?"

"The box has a false bottom and it is heavy when empty. The icon must be in it."

Claudette went on to explain her reasons while Pierre listened.

"The key?"

"It is nothing, a hairpin could turn the lock."

Pierre drew in a long breath.

"Now we must think, sugar."

"You think, my treasure, I am taking a shower. We have a long night before us."

"And we have another six days. This mustn't be rushed."

"At least, they are paying tonight," Claudette said as she began to undress.

After a splendid dinner at the Tour d'Argent, they all went to the Lido, that glamorous musical show on the Champs-Elysées.

Although Lepski was impressed with the magnificent view from the restaurant's windows of the flood-lit Notre Dame, he proved difficult when Pierre proposed the famous pressed duck. Lepski said he didn't dig fancy food, and he would have a steak.

"You will have nothing of the kind!" Carroll snapped. "You are in Paris, and you must take advantage of the beautiful food."

112

"Can't a guy eat what he likes?" Lepski grumbled.

"We will have the duck," Carroll said firmly.

When the duck was served, Lepski tried it suspiciously, then declared, "This isn't bad! Look, baby, you must try this when we get home." He turned to Pierre, "Carroll is a marvellous cook."

"Eat it and be quiet!" Carroll snapped.

Finally, the dinner finished, Lepski flicked his fingers for the check. He paled visibly when he saw what the dinner had cost, and paled again when he asked Pierre what tip he should leave. He counted out the French banknotes, muttering to himself, then with a croaking laugh, said to Pierre, "This little joint sure won't go bankrupt," and got a sharp kick on his shin from Carroll.

But the show girls at the Lido lifted his depression, and when they finally returned to the hotel, around 02.00, Lepski said it had been a great day.

"Tomorrow will be your last day in Paris," Pierre said as they all went up in the elevator to their rooms. "I suggest we visit the Left Bank and take a walk around the old quarters. There is much of interest to see, then you must go to the Folies Bergère: more girls and a great show. I suggest we dine at the Grand Vefour, another of Paris's greats. This will be on us, Tom."

Lepski visibly brightened, but Carroll would have none of it.

"It is on *us*!" she said firmly. "We insist." She ignored Lepski's faint moan.

There was a friendly argument as they walked to their rooms, but Pierre, knowing what the check for the following evening would come to, graciously accepted that they would be the Lepskis' guests.

While Lepski was protesting in their room, telling Carroll she was out of her mind to throw their money around in this way, the Duvines, in their room, regarded each other.

"I had a terrible feeling," Claudette said, "they would let you pay for tomorrow. We must save our expenses, my treasure."

Pierre patted her.

"I knew she would insist. I wouldn't have suggested the

113

Grand Vefour if I hadn't been sure." He smiled lovingly at his wife. "Are you enjoying all this?"

"If we could only live like this forever!" Claudette began to undress. "Have you been thinking?"

"Of course. We can't do a thing until we get to Montreux. I am still wondering how I can contact Radnitz. This is the problem, sugar."

"We have six days. Are you tired?"

"Not too tired," Pierre said, looking at her nakedness with adoring eyes, and began hurriedly to undress.

At Zurich airport, a tall thin man with straw-coloured hair, neatly trimmed to his collar, wearing a dark blue business suit, carrying a suitcase, moved with the passengers just off the New York flight towards the Swiss passport control. As the queue moved forward, he saw there were two men in plain clothes standing behind the passport official, and guessed they were security police.

When his turn came, he presented his passport. The three men eyed him.

"Are you here on business, Mr Holtz?" the passport official asked.

"No. I am visiting friends," Sergas Holtz replied in his cold, clipped German. "I will only be here for a week."

"Have a pleasant visit."

Sergas Holtz moved into the customs shed. There was a long queue of exasperated passengers, waiting while several grey uniformed customs men dealt with their baggage.

With a sardonic little smile, Holtz waited patiently. He thought all this effort and delay for nothing slightly amusing. Finally, his turn came. He opened his suitcase and watched the official search, his fingers tracing around the inside of the case, and Holtz was thankful he hadn't had to bring the vanity box through this customs' check.

"Thank you, sir," the official said, and leaving Holtz to replace his things into the case, moved on to the next passenger.

Holtz walked to the Hertz desk. With his Hertz credit card, he was quickly provided with a Ford Escort. He asked for a street guide of the city which was handed to him.

His uncle had given him two addresses. Sitting in the rented car, he tracked down the addresses on the map, then headed for the centre of the city.

The first address was a shabby apartment block not far from the airport. He found parking space with difficulty, then entered the building, took the creaking elevator to the third floor and rang the bell of a heavy oak front door.

The door opened, after a delay, and a small bearded man in his late sixties, dressed in a grey flannel shirt and dark brown corduroy trousers, peered suspiciously at him from behind thick-lensed glasses.

"Mr Frederick?" Holtz asked.

"Yes."

"You are expecting me." Holtz offered his passport.

Frederick examined the passport closely, grunted and handed it back. He stood aside.

"Come in, Mr. Holtz."

Holtz entered a dark lobby, then followed Frederick into a large living room, furnished with heavy, ugly furniture.

"I am here to serve you," Frederick said. "I have had many pleasant dealings with your uncle. What can I do for you?"

"A pistol," Holtz said. "A Beretta if you have one."

"Ah! That's a beautiful weapon, only weighing ten ounces and only four and a half inches long."

"I know that!" Holtz said impatiently. "Have you one?"

"Yes. It is almost new, and in perfect condition. It costs . . ."

"I am not interested in what it costs. You will charge it to my uncle," Holtz said curtly. "Let me see it."

"In a few moments."

Frederick left the room, closing the door behind him. Holtz went to the window, drew aside the net curtain and looked down into the street. His hard eyes surveyed the passing people, the crawling cars. He saw nothing suspicious, but suspicion was ingrained in his nature. He dropped the curtain and moved to the centre of the room as Frederick came in, carrying a cardboard box.

"There are twenty five rounds of ammunition," he said, setting the box down on the table. "I fear I have no more."

"They will be enough." Holtz opened the box, took out the gun, lying in cotton wool, and examined it. His examination was searching and expert.

"I see you understand guns," Frederick said, watching. "You will find it in perfect order."

Holtz ignored the remark. Satisfied with the gun, he opened the box of ammunition, and after scrutinising each bullet, he loaded the gun.

"I'll take it," he said. "Now, I want a hunting knife."

"Certainly, Mr Holtz. I will fetch my best selection."

Again Frederick left the room and returned some minutes later with a large box which he set on the table. Removing the lid, he said, "Please make your selection."

Holtz took nearly half an hour examining the collection of knives before he made his choice.

"This one," he said, holding up a murderous-looking knife with a flat ebony handle and a razor-sharp blade some four inches long.

"An excellent choice. The best knife I have in my collection," Frederick said. "There is a sheath to go with it." He rummaged in the box and produced a soft sheath in deerskin with straps.

Holtz put the knife into the sheath, then pulling up his right trouser leg, he strapped the knife into place. After a little adjustment, he found the knife lay snugly against the fleshy part of his calf. Pulling down the trouser leg, he walked around the room, then nodded.

"I'll take it. Charge it to my uncle," and with barely a nod, he walked out of the living-room, opened the front door and took the elevator down to the entrance of the apartment block, the Beretta in his hip pocket, the box of ammunition in his jacket pocket, the knife strapped to his leg.

Since he had left New York, completely unarmed, Holtz had felt naked, but not now. He walked with an assured step to his car, got in, paused to check the map, then set off to the second address.

He had some difficulty with the one-way streets and the heavy, slow-moving traffic, but eventually he came upon a pair of gates with a plaque bearing the number he was seeking. He drove into the yard.

A few minutes later, he stood in a handsomely furnished office, shaking hands with a tall, balding Swiss who introduced himself as Herr Weidmann.

"Your uncle telephoned, Mr Holtz. It is always a great pleasure to do something for him. The box is ready. I can assure you everything is as your uncle has ordered."

Holtz nodded.

"I am pressed for time," he said curtly. "Give me the box."

Weidmann's smile slipped. He wasn't used to such abrupt treatment, nor did he like the look of this tall, thin man with his hard, probing eyes.

"Certainly, certainly." He went to a cupboard, unlocked it and took out the blue vanity box. "It is a perfect replica. You will see from the photographs . . ."

"Have it wrapped!" Holtz barked. "I am in a hurry!"

Weidmann took the box and left the office. What an uncouth fellow, he thought as his secretary wrapped the box. Who would believe he was Gustav Holtz's nephew?

He returned with the parcel and Holtz took it from him.

"I can assure you everything has been carried out, according to Mr Holtz's instructions," Weidmann said, forcing a smile. "There is . . ."

"Okay, I'll take it as read," Holtz said, and turning, left the office and walked back to his car.

Now for Radnitz's villa.

The journey to Villa Helios took time. Holtz was exasperated by the heavy, crawling traffic, but he was careful to control his impatience. It wouldn't do to have a collision, but there were moments when he had to contain his vicious temper not to shout at the drivers who tried to edge in on him, tried to beat the traffic lights, tried to force their way out of side streets.

It was a little after 16.00 when he eventually pulled up outside the impressive portals of the villa, although Holtz was not impressed. The way rich tycoons put on a show of wealth bored him. As he mounted the marble steps, he wondered how anyone could live in such an ostentatious style.

Mythen opened the front door and gave him a little bow.

"Mr. Holtz?"

"Yes." Holtz regarded the old man with contempt: a born lackey, a boot licker, he thought.

"Please come in. Mr Radnitz is engaged, but he will see you in a little while."

Holtz followed the old man into a large room furnished with priceless antiques.

"Perhaps coffee, tea or a drink of some kind while you wait, Mr Holtz?" Mythen inquired.

"Nothing!" Holtz snapped, and crossing the room to the window, he gazed out at the vast expanse of lawn, the trees, the flowering shrubs and the big swimming pool.

Mythen quietly withdrew, closing the door behind him.

Holtz remained at the window. After some minutes, he saw a powerfully built man, wearing a black jogging suit, move across the lawn. He was followed by two other men of the same build and wearing similar clothes. They all disappeared behind a high bank of flowering shrubs. Holtz registered this with a sardonic grin. Radnitz's bodyguards, he thought. Well, they looked efficient. He supposed a man in Radnitz's position automatically wasted money on bodyguards more for self-esteem than protection.

Half an hour later, Mythen came to the door.

"Mr Radnitz will now see you. Please follow me."

Carrying the wrapped vanity box, Holtz walked behind Mythen to Radnitz's study.

Radnitz, seated behind his paper-strewn desk, a cigar between his fat fingers, regarded this tall, thin man as he came into the room with searching interest. He watched Holtz's cat-like walk as he moved towards his desk.

Radnitz, an astute judge of men, came to the immediate conclusion that this man could match up to Lu Silk's standards. Since Gustav Holtz had recommended him, Radnitz had no misgivings, but he wanted to see for himself.

In his turn, Holtz regarded Radnitz. Yes, he thought, this was a man he could co-operate with. His uncle's description of the power, the ruthlessness of Herman Radnitz was no exaggeration.

"You have the vanity box?" Radnitz asked in his hard, guttural voice.

"Yes, sir." Holtz placed the parcel on the desk.

118

"Is it satisfactory?"

"That I don't know. Weidmann who made it said it was. He and my uncle discussed it. I was only told to bring it to you. I haven't checked it out."

"If your uncle is satisfied, I am." Radnitz puffed at his cigar. "Sit down."

Holtz sat in a chair near Radnitz's desk.

"You are now a member of my staff," Radnitz said. "Your uncle has guaranteed you. Has he explained your duties?"

Holtz inclined his head.

"You may have nothing to do for weeks, then you could get an assignment. You are always to be within reach. You will keep me informed where I can contact you at a moment's notice. Understood?"

Again Holtz inclined his head.

"You are, from now on, my hit-man as they call killers. Your uncle has told you the terms of payment. Are you satisfied?"

"Yes, sir."

"You have no hesitation accepting this job?"

A faint bored expression came into Holtz's eyes.

"Why should I, sir?"

"You understand your immediate task?"

"My uncle told me I was to go to the Montreux Palace hotel at Montreux and exchange this vanity box for a similar one owned by a Mrs Lepski."

"That is correct. How are you going to do this?"

"The Lepskis will be arriving at the hotel in six days' time. I will arrive two days before they arrive. My uncle has already reserved a room for me on the same floor as their reservation. I will wait my opportunity, then make the exchange."

"You think you can do this?"

Again the faintly bored expression came into Holtz's eyes.

"I wouldn't be here, sir, unless I was certain."

Radnitz liked this confidence. He nodded approvingly.

"When you get Mrs Lepski's box, you are to bring it without delay to me here."

"I understand, sir."

"You have three days before leaving for Montreux. A

room has been reserved for you at the Eden hotel. What will you do while waiting to leave?"

"Learn to open hotel bedroom doors," Holtz said. "My uncle has given me the name of a locksmith who will teach me. This is something I have to learn. Unless I can open Mrs Lepski's bedroom door, I wouldn't be able to get the box."

Radnitz nodded.

"Your uncle is a remarkable man. He thinks of everything. I trust you will come up to his standards."

"Yes, sir."

"Very well. You are now at liberty to do what you think necessary. I will expect you here with Mrs Lepski's box within a week. Should you fail, I will have no further use for you. Understand?"

"Yes, sir," and Holtz stood up.

"I am told by your uncle that you are very able to take care of yourself," Radnitz said with a sly little grin. "Although I usually take your uncle's opinions seriously, I also prefer sometimes to check out these opinions. Have you any objections to a test as to how well you can take care of yourself?"

Holtz's eyes turned cloudy.

"Why should I?" he asked in a cold, flat voice.

"Then do me a favour of taking a walk down to the lake." Radnitz waved towards the open French windows. "I would like to see for myself if you can take care of yourself."

"If that is what you want, sir, then, of course, I will do what you ask." Holtz paused and stared at Radnitz. "I take it the three goons who are probably your bodyguards and who are hiding in that distant clump of shrubs will attempt to rough me up for your amusement. That is understandable, sir, but I should tell you I don't play rough games. Before I go out there, I must ask you if you have anywhere convenient to bury those three goons?"

Radnitz stiffened.

"Bury them? What do you mean?"

Holtz bent, lifted his right trouser leg and the glittering bladed knife jumped into his hand. The movement was so swift Radnitz sat motionless, his frog-like eyes wide open.

"You see, sir, I don't play rough games. When three

powerful men attempt to crowd me, I cut them," Holtz said quietly. A sardonic smile twitched at his lips. "You wouldn't employ them unless you had faith in them to guard you. It seems a waste to lose them, but it would also be a nuisance for one of your servants to bury them. I don't undertake burials. I only undertake elimination." He stared at Radnitz, his eyes vicious. "Do you still wish me to take a walk down to the lake, sir?"

For a long moment, Radnitz sat still, staring at this man and at the murderous knife in his hand, then he recovered himself.

"Under the circumstances, I think a test is unnecessary," he said. "Go and learn how to unlock hotel bedroom doors, go to the Montreux Palace hotel and return with the box."

"It is as you wish, sir," Holtz said, returning the knife into its sheath, then picking up the parcel, giving Radnitz a slight nod, he left the room.

Radnitz stubbed out his cigar. He felt slightly shaken. It was as if Death had walked out of the room, and Radnitz feared death: the only thing he did fear.

seven

Lu Bradey uttered a groan of despair as he saw Maggie Schultz enter the Kennedy airport check-in lobby, followed by a coloured porter pushing a trolley on which were two large suitcases and a blue vanity box.

He reached her in four long strides.

"What are you thinking of?" he demanded. "I told you to travel light for God's sake!"

Maggie Schultz was something very special in women. She caused a male sensation wherever she went. Even now, with the check-in desk busy, male heads turned, and there were even a few suppressed whistles.

Maggie was not only beautiful in every possible way, but sex oozed from her the way treacle oozes from a can. Blonde, with thick silky hair, her body was so perfectly built fashion photographers, *Playboy*, *Penthouse* and, of course, porn specialists scrambled for her. Her face carried a please-help-me expression that raised male blood pressure.

"There you are, pet," she cried, and throwing her arms around Bradey, gave him a kiss that caused the male audience to sigh with envy.

Bradey shoved her away.

"All this goddamn luggage! Didn't I tell you . . ."

She put her hand over his mouth.

"Baby, you don't expect me to walk around Switzerland naked, do you?"

"Okay, okay." Bradey contained his exasperation. "Now you know what to do? Check in, take the box and go through the customs. If they ask questions tell them you are going to join friends in Geneva. Remember?"

"Yes, pet. Will this nice man take care of the rest of the luggage?"

"He'll see you through the customs. I'll meet you in the departure lounge."

She kissed him again, then went over to the check-in desk and presented her ticket.

Bradey watched her finally join the queue for the baggage search.

The customs officer eyed Maggie as she came to rest before him. Man! he thought, what wouldn't I give to drag this piece into my bed!

Maggie, reading his thoughts, gave him a big sexy smile. "Tell me, handsome, are you married?" she asked.

The customs officer blinked, then grinned.

"Sure, I guess I am."

"I'm so glad. You are going to search my baggage, aren't you? Young bachelors always embarrass me. Us girls just have to take things with us, but a nice married man understands." She presented him with a set of keys. "Do be kind and open the bags for me. I'm plain stupid with locks."

Taking the keys, the customs officer leered at her.

"I bet you're not stupid about other things, miss," he said as the porter put the bags on the counter.

"Oh, I am. I'm just dizzy." Maggie rolled her beautiful sea-green eyes. "My mother said I was born with a body, but no brains. Wasn't that a terrible thing to say, but she was right."

The customs officer unlocked the bags.

"I wouldn't know, miss, but she was certainly right about one thing," he said as he began to go through the contents of the bags, careful not to disarrange anything.

Bradey, standing at the end of the queue, watched all this. He could see Maggie was talking and laughing and oozing sex, and he was glad he had brought her. He watched the customs officer open the vanity box, but as Maggie was still talking, his search was perfunctory. It occurred to Bradey that Maggie could certainly have smuggled out the icon had it been in the box. He told himself he must use Maggie's sexual charms more often in the future.

He watched Maggie take the box, give the customs officer a wide smile and pass on to the departure lounge. The coloured porter took her bags and carried them away to the trolley waiting to be loaded.

Twenty minutes later, Bradey joined Maggie.

"He was the sweetest thing," Maggie said. "Oh, I am so enjoying all this! And now Switzerland! Baby, this is the first time I have gone to Europe!"

At the age of thirteen, Maggie had seduced one of her school teachers who had gone to jail, and she had been put "into care." She had run away six months later from the home, and was taken up by an elderly, rich man who liked young, pretty girls. He passed her off as his granddaughter. She had remained with him until she was fifteen, then bored with his constant demands, she took up with a coloured man who had a string of girls. She did a six months stint of street walking which she found dreary and unprofitable, not to say dangerous. She then moved to Florida where for the next two years she did "call girl" service and made a considerable amount of money which she spent, living in the kind of luxury which, at her age, satisfied her. She then met an advertising executive who immediately realized her potential. He took her to New York and introduced her to a number of his friends who got her assignments for fashion photography. She was in and out of their beds until she reached the age of twenty-one. Then she met Lu Bradey and fell in love with him: an experience that had never happened to her before. Bradey had explained to her that he was in the antique furniture business and had to do a lot of travelling, but it was okay with him if she liked to move into his West Side apartment and expect him when she saw him. He also advised her to continue with her fashion work as he was not rich enough to support the two of them. Love was such a wonderful thing to Maggie that she agreed. For the next six months she saw

Bradey some ten times. He always seemed rushed. Maggie never asked questions. She was happy to see him when she saw him and she kept his apartment tidy, cooked for him when he returned home and continued to make good money with her free-lance modelling. Then suddenly he had telephoned her to say he was going to Switzerland and would she like to come with him? Nearly out of her mind with joy, Maggie screamed, "Try and stop me!"

He came around the following evening with her air ticket and the blue vanity box. This was the first present Bradey had ever given her and she smothered him with kisses. Bradey refrained from telling her the box wouldn't remain in her possession for long.

The flight from New York to Geneva came up to Maggie's expectations. They travelled first class, and Bradey, from long experience, quickly captured the attention of one of the air hostesses who kept them both supplied with champagne, canapés and later, dry vodka martinis.

Arriving at Geneva airport, Bradey left Maggie to go through the customs with her baggage and vanity box. He had with him a small overnight case and was quickly through the customs search. He then went over to the Hertz desk and organised a Mercedes car.

There was some delay before Maggie appeared.

"I don't think I am going to like the Swiss," she said. "The horrid man wouldn't unlock my bags and made me take everything out."

"The vanity box?"

"That too. Everyone was staring at my things. He was a horrid brute."

"Never mind. The car's waiting. Come on," and signalling to a porter who piled the luggage on a trolley, Bradey conducted Maggie to where the Mercedes was parked. As he drove on to the autoroute and headed towards the city, he thought maybe Maggie's sexual charms might not be so useful if he had ever to smuggle something through the Swiss customs.

On the other side of the Atlantic, in Paradise City, Claude Kendrick and Louis de Marney were discussing their future.

"With all this money, Claude my brave," Louis was saying, "why not sell the Gallery and retire? Think of what you could do with almost three million dollars. Think of the life of freedom you will be able to enjoy. If the price is right, I would be willing to buy the Gallery from you with my share of the money. What do you think?"

"That you are out of your tiny mind," Kendrick said. "You haven't the first idea how much this gallery is worth. You? You couldn't even run it without me."

"Oh, I might." Louis's rat-like eyes hardened. "I'd be prepared to take the risk. How about half a million, pet?"

"This room alone is worth more than that," Kendrick said, making a sweeping movement with his hand towards the pictures and the antiques. "Now, stop it, Louis or I will get cross with you. I have no intention of selling the Gallery to you or anyone else. Tomorrow, I have to fly to Zurich. How I hate flying!"

"Have you made a will?" Louis asked, his expression cunning. "You must have! Think of all the dreadful accidents! Every day I read of air crashes!"

"If you don't get out of this room immediately, I will throw something at you!" Kendrick exclaimed, his fat face flushing.

"I'm only trying to be helpful. There is no point in you getting into a tizz. You mustn't excite yourself. It's bad for your liver."

As Kendrick reached for a heavy paperweight, Louis scuttled to the door and disappeared, slamming the door behind him.

Kendrick glowered at the door, then lighting a cigar, he thought of tomorrow. He had had reassuring news from Haddon. The Lepskis' vanity box had passed through the French customs. The Lepskis and the Duvines were now in Monaco, and in another three days, they would be at the Montreux Palace hotel. Haddon had said that Lu Bradey would be at this hotel and he would get the box from Duvine, then would go to Zurich as soon as he could, meeting Kendrick at the Eden hotel. So far so good, but Kendrick was a pessimist. He never believed in infallibilities. Maybe the Swiss customs would check the box and find the icon. Maybe Bradey would have a car accident on his way from Montreux to Zurich.

Maybe, and here Kendrick broke out into a cold sweat, his plane might plunge into the Atlantic. Life was never free of problems. Then maybe that dreadful man Radnitz might try to gyp him out of the three million dollars. When dealing with Radnitz, anything could happen. He took out his silk handkerchief and mopped his forehead. He would have been even more uneasy if he could have transported himself to the entrance to the Montreux Palace hotel right at that moment.

The uniformed porter ran down the steps to open the door of an Opel Rekord car as it pulled up outside the Montreux Palace hotel.

A tall, thin man with straw-coloured hair looked at the porter through the open car window.

"My bag's in the boot," he said curtly. "Do I park over there?"

"If you will, sir," the porter said, went around to the back of the car and took out a large suitcase which was surprisingly light for its size.

Sergas Holtz drove into a parking slot, then getting out of the car, climbed the steps and walked over to the reception desk.

His uncle had given him a false passport in the name of Hans Richter which he handed to the reception clerk.

"Glad to have you here, sir," the clerk said. "You are staying a few days?"

"Yes," Holtz said curtly as the clerk filled in the police card which he handed to Holtz with a pen. Holtz signed his false name. "Friends of mine, Mr and Mrs Lepski, are arriving the day after tomorrow. What is the number of their room?"

The clerk consulted the register.

"Room 245, sir. You have room 249. It's quite close."

Holtz nodded, then walked with the porter to the elevator. Once in his room, he locked the door, put the suitcase on the bed, opened it and took the vanity box from it. This he put in a closet, locked the door and dropped the key into his pocket.

He crossed to the window and looked down at the busy street below, then across the lake and to the range of mountains.

128

Well, he thought, I have arrived. Two days to wait, then action!

The drive down to the South of France on the long, monotonous autoroute du Sud had bored the Lepskis, although Carroll was too polite to say so, realising how the Duvines were trying to please, but Lepski made grumbling noises until she told him firmly to be quiet. They both had expected better things than this continous flat countryside, the traffic congested, narrow-streeted towns and the dreary, dirty-looking little villages. Even the ★★★ Pic hotel at Valence where they spent the night, Lepski found too goddamn fussy, and this time, after listening impatiently to Pierre who enthusiastically translated the luxe menu, he declared firmly he would have a steak, and gave Carroll his cop stare, challenging her to say otherwise. Seeing the danger signal, Carroll didn't argue.

They had arrived at the Metropole hotel, Monte Carlo, the following afternoon. Here again, they were disillusioned. Carroll had read so much about the South of France with its constant sunshine, its villas, casinos, smart shops and quaint old towns. She found to her dismay Monte Carlo was cramped, over-built with half-empty high-risers and mainly fat old people moving along the sidewalks. The shops proved an anti-climax after the Paris shops.

In spite of Pierre working desperately, they found Monte Carlo a drag. By now even Carroll had had enough of the rich French cuisine, and she and Lepski would only eat BBQ chicken or steaks. This depressed the Duvines who were always prepared for an elaborate meal.

Lepski was amazed to find the streets of Monte Carlo deserted, except for parked cars, by 21.00. The only apparent night life was at the Casino. There, he found the aged fat women, gambling, with fat men hovering around them, depressing. There wasn't a sexy-looking girl to be seen. Pierre had explained that the season was nearly over. Had Lepski come a month earlier, he would have seen plenty of glamour. Lepski didn't believe him.

On the last night of their stay at the Metropole hotel after dining in the roof restaurant of the Hotel de Paris, Lepski

129

and Carroll lay in the twin beds in their room. They had been so bored with the Casino which Pierre and Claudette had suggested after dinner, that they had opted for an early night as they would be driving to Montreux the following morning.

The Duvines, born gamblers, had gone to the Casino where they had lost, between them, over a thousand francs.

"Are you enjoying this trip?" Lepski asked abruptly.

Carroll hesitated. She believed in always telling the truth.

"Well, Tom, I thought it was going to be more exciting," she said finally. "I loved Paris, and I'm glad to have come this far. I wouldn't have known what it really is like if I hadn't come, would I?"

"Yeah." Lepski moved restlessly, "But if we hadn't come, think of the money we could have saved."

"It is *my* money, and I spend it how I like!" Carroll snapped.

"Sure, sure," Lepski said hurriedly.

"You wait until we get to Switzerland. I've seen photos of the mountains and the lakes . . . marvellous!"

"Any night life there?"

"Of course!" Carroll said firmly, hoping there would be. "A place like Montreux will be alive with night life. There's one thing you are forgetting, Tom, we have found two real, lovely friends. Claudette promised to write when I get home. She will be a pen pal."

"Oh, yeah? There's something about those two that bothers me."

Carroll sat up.

"What do you mean?"

"There's a touch of the con-man about Pierre. He's too goddamn smooth. I keep asking myself why he is taking all this trouble, spending money on us, driving us two Americans out of the blue. I get a feeling before long he'll try to sell us a gold-mine."

"Lepski! You are utterly impossible! You have a horrid cop mind! If someone is nice and friendly to you, you immediately think he's a crook! I'm ashamed of you!" Carroll declared furiously. "How do you imagine people make friends? Because they like each other! The Duvines like us,

130

so they are our friends. Can't you get that into your narrow cop mind?"

Lepski moaned. Here was another fight coming up that could last for hours, and he was tired.

"Okay, okay, baby. I guess it's my cop training and my narrow mind," he said, pulling up the sheet and settling lower in the bed. "Let's sleep, huh? We have quite a trip ahead of us tomorrow."

Carroll drew in an exasperated breath.

"It's always 'Okay, okay, baby,' when you won't discuss anything. Let me tell you, Lepski, the Duvines are marvellous people, and we are very, very lucky to have found them!"

Lepski made a soft snoring noise.

"Do you hear what I am saying?" Carroll demanded.

"Sure, baby. Sleep tight," Lepski mumbled in a feigned sleepy voice and began to snore at volume.

Pierre and Claudette returned to the hotel soon after 01.30. They were both depressed at losing money at roulette.

In their room, after showers, they lay in the twin beds in the half-light of one bedside lamp.

"No luck tonight," Pierre said gloomily.

"We can't always win, my treasure," Claudette said. "What worries me is the Lepskis are getting bored."

"Americans! Most of them can't adapt to the European way of life. Not much longer, sugar. On the 20th, we will be in Montreux. Lu will be there to give me the duplicate box. As soon as I get it, you will take the Lepskis on a boat trip. When Lu has given me the duplicate box, he takes off for Zurich to wait for me. As soon as he's gone, I will switch boxes. When you return with the Lepskis, I will tell them I've had a cable saying my mother is dangerously ill and we must return to Paris immediately. Once we are shot of the Lepskis, we will drive to Zurich and get in touch with Radnitz."

"But will we get shot of the Lepskis? Suppose they say they will return to Paris with us?"

Pierre frowned.

"A good point. We must find out what their plans are after Montreux. Let's sell them on the idea of going to Gstaad.

131

You do that, sugar. Talk to Carroll and tell her they can't possibly leave Switzerland without seeing Gstaad."

"Yes. Then, another thing, when we don't arrive at the Eden, Zurich, Lu will know we've double-crossed him. He could make things difficult."

There was a long silence while Pierre thought, then he said, "First things first. This is the general plan. Get the Lepskis thinking of Gstaad. I have to get the icon."

Claudette leaned out of her bed and stroked Pierre's hand.

"I hate twin beds."

"There's room in here with me," Pierre said and threw back the blanket and sheet.

Claudette slid from her bed and into his, and wound her arms lovingly around him.

Lu Bradey and Maggie Schultz walked into the reception lobby of the Montreux Palace hotel, followed by a porter, carrying their luggage.

It was 11:30 on the 18th September: a bright, crispy autumn morning. Driving from Geneva, along the lakeside road, Maggie had been entranced by the view of Lake Léman, the mountains and the acres of vineyards. The entrance to the hotel also entranced her. She thought the luggage porter a dream, and the reception clerk out of this world.

"We are only staying two nights," Bradey said as he handed the reception clerk the false passport Ed Haddon had given him in the name of Lewis Schultz.

"Yes, sir, I have your reservation."

"I want to book a room for my friend who will be arriving on the afternoon of the 20th," Bradey said. "Mr John Willis. He will be staying a few days."

"Mr Willis? Certainly, sir. At this time we have plenty of room." The clerk made a note.

"I believe you have Mr and Mrs Lepski booked in here on the 20th?"

"Mr and Mrs Lepski?" The clerk checked the register. "That is correct. They are with Mr and Mrs Duvine."

"Mr Willis is an old friend. I would like him to be on their floor."

The clerk checked, then nodded.

132

"Perfectly all right, sir. Room 251. Mr and Mrs Lepski will be occupying room 245. If you are leaving on the morning of the 20th, and Mr Willis will be arriving after lunch, you can have this room. Would that be convenient?"

"That's fine."

Sergas Holtz, sitting in the reception lobby, pretending to be reading *The Herald Tribune*, was very much alert. He had been sitting in the reception lobby for more than an hour, waiting developments. He had stiffened slightly as he saw the porter bring in the baggage of these arrivals. He saw the blue vanity box, the twin of the box he had locked in the closet in his room.

So this is Bradey, he thought. His uncle had explained to him that Bradey would arrive with a duplicate of the box and would give it to Duvine to switch with Lepski's box. But who was this John Willis Bradey was talking about? Another complication?

Up in room 251, having tipped the porter, Bradey joined Maggie on the balcony.

"Isn't this gorgeous!" Maggie exclaimed. "Oh, let's explore! Look at that cute steamer! I'd love to go on it! What a cute little town!"

"Maggie," Bradey said quietly. "Let's sit down. I want to talk to you."

Maggie looked at him, her eyes startled.

"Why, of course, sweetheart. Is something wrong?"

They re-entered the room and sat down.

"I am in the pipe-line to make a million dollars," Bradey said, knowing money was his wisest opening move.

"*A million dollars!*" Maggie exclaimed. "You can't mean it!"

"Look, baby, it's better for you not to know anything about it, but it is a fact: one million dollars." Bradey smiled. "How would you like to marry me?"

"You and a million dollars? Try and stop me! I'd adore it!"

Bradey suppressed a sigh. He wondered what her reaction would have been if he hadn't mentioned the million dollars.

"Fine! As soon as we get home, baby, we'll get married, but to get this money, I need your help."

133

"You have only to tell me, Lu. Just tell me how I can help."

"We leave here the day after tomorrow. We will drive along the lake road to Villeneuve: not far. There, I will leave you. You will take the car and drive to Zurich and stay at the Baur au Lac hotel. I will join you in less than a week."

"Drive to Zurich?" Maggie's voice shot up. "But, Lu, I couldn't. I..."

"There's nothing to it," Bradey said patiently. He took from his wallet a folded piece of paper. "Here's your route. It's simple. Here's a street plan showing you how to find the hotel. A room is reserved for you." He pulled his chair closer. "Let's go through it together."

After a quarter of an hour, Maggie said doubtfully that she thought she could find her way.

"But can't I stay with you?" she asked plaintively. "Must I go on my own?"

"If you want me and a million dollars, you have to go!" Bradey said, a snap in his voice.

"What will you do?"

"Earn a million dollars: something you don't want to know about." From his hip pocket, he took a wallet and handed it to her. "These are blank traveller's cheques: worth fifteen thousand Swiss francs. Have yourself a ball in Zurich while you wait for me. Okay?"

"All this for me?"

"Yes, but you will have to take care of your hotel bill. Okay?"

Maggie gave a squeal of delight.

"You are the sweetest of the sweetest!"

"Fine." Bradey nodded. "One more thing. The vanity box. I need that. When you are in Zurich, buy yourself another. Right?"

Maggie's sea-green eyes popped wide open.

"Oh, no! It is the first present you have ever given me! I adore it! You can't have it!"

Bradey had been anticipating her opposition. He gave her his con-smile.

"I need it, baby. Now, you and I will go out right now and we will go to one of the best watch shops and I will

134

buy you a beautiful watch to make up for the vanity box; self-winding, solid gold with diamonds. How's that?"

"Solid gold with diamonds, and I can buy another vanity box?"

Bradey smiled at her.

"That's what the man said."

Maggie jumped to her feet; her eyes sparkling with excitement.

"Let's go!" She rushed to the door, then paused. "Then can we go on that steamer?"

"We'll even do that," Bradey said.

They rode down in the elevator, and watched by Sergas Holtz, they walked out into the sunshine, arm in arm, and headed for the nearest Omega watch shop.

Happily for Bradey, Maggie was easy to please. She adored going to Evian on the steamer. She adored wandering down the narrow main street where the shops were. She peered at all the shop windows, and when she wasn't doing that, she was adoring her new watch. Bradey, thinking of the million dollars he was going to earn, wandered with her, bored stupid.

In the evening they visited the Montreux casino and Maggie won twenty francs which sent her out of her mind with delight. He took her to Hazyland where they danced among the young, and Maggie caused wolf whistles which she loved. They had wild sex when they returned to their room and they slept.

The following morning, Bradey drove her to see Noel Coward's old home. Maggie adored the mountains and the drive. She got out of the car, outside Coward's entrance, to gape. Sitting in the car, Bradey, although his mind was occupied with the task ahead, watched her and told himself, he could do a hell of a lot worse than marrying this beauty.

After lunch at Le Cygne, the Montreux Palace hotel's grillroom, Maggie pleaded to go on a steamer again. They took the trip to Lausanne and returned to the hotel in time for dinner.

So the day passed. Maggie declared she adored everything. As she lay in his arms, sleeping, Bradey thought of tomorrow. Duvine, with the Lepskis, would be arriving. He hoped they wouldn't be late. This operation was a matter of timing. He slept badly that night.

To avoid the Italian customs and a major Swiss customs frontier, Duvine had driven via Grenoble, by-passing Geneva and driving along Lake Léman on the French side of the lake to the Swiss frontier outside St Gingolph.

The Lepskis, who had lived all their lives in Florida, had never seen mountains as big and as impressive as they saw on the route de Napoléon. Even Lepski was impressed. Carroll was ecstatic.

"Tom!" she cried. "Just look at this view! It's worth the rest of our trip!"

Duvine sighed with relief. Well, at least, something was pleasing these difficult two.

"Well, yeah," Lepski said grudgingly. "I guess it's pretty good, but our Rocky mountains are as good."

"Lepski! Since when have you ever seen the Rocky mountains? Don't show your ignorance!" Carroll said scathingly.

"Well, we've got the Grand Canyon too," Lepski said defensively. "That wants some beating."

"Since when have you seen the Grand Canyon?"

Lepski made a noise like a fall of gravel, and Claudette broke in hurriedly. "We'll be coming to Lake Léman. One side is Swiss, the other side is French. Isn't that a nice arrangement?"

"How cute!" Carroll said. "You know, Claudette, I'm just loving all this."

"When do we eat?" Lepski asked.

"There's a little restaurant not far from here," Duvine said. He had given up trying to please these two with good food. Why waste money on them, he reasoned to himself, when all they wanted was a goddamn steak?

Although the Duvines enjoyed their curried scampi, the Lepskis found their steaks tough.

"We should have brought along your mincer, baby," Lepski said, chewing hard. "Then we could have had ground meat."

Carroll told him to be quiet.

Half an hour's drive would bring them to the Swiss frontier and Duvine, knowing it was the last hurdle to cross, had to control his uneasiness.

"Swiss officials can be awkward," he said to Lepski as they drove along the lake road. "Leave them to me. I'll tell them that you are a distinguished American police officer. They could make us open our bags. The trick with them is to give them a bone. We'll stop at the next village and buy some Scotch which we will declare."

Lepski brightened.

"Scotch? That's a great idea!"

They stopped at a wine merchant just before the frontier, and bought two bottles of Scotch and two bottles of champagne.

"This should do it," Duvine said, putting the bottles in the boot of the car. Looking at the luggage, seeing the blue vanity box very much in evidence, he was inspired to move it close to his own luggage and pull his and Claudette's coats over it, leaving the Lepskis' new-looking luggage exposed.

He got back into the car and drove down the narrow street leading to the French customs post. His hands were moist and his mouth was dry.

The French customs guard waved them through. They drove the few yards towards the Swiss customs post.

Two tall, grey-uniformed men moved out into the street.

"Leave all this to me," Duvine said as he wound down his window.

Lepski became alert. His police training told him that Duvine was unnaturally tense, and this puzzled him. He wondered why Duvine was making such a thing of this. He told himself to relax. Duvine must know from experience what he was about. He handed Carroll's and his passports to Duvine who, with his own, gave the guard a friendly nod and offered the passports.

The guard regarded him with cold, stony eyes, then stepping back, examined the passports. These, after a long scrutiny, he handed back.

"Have you anything to declare?" he asked in French.

"No, nothing. Two bottles of whisky and two champagne: nothing else," Duvine said.

"Open your boot please."

"What's he say?" Lepski demanded, irritated that the conversation was in French.

"He wants me to open the boot," Duvine told him as he got out of the car.

· "Why?"

"They do," Duvine said curtly, wishing to God Lepski would keep quiet.

He went around to the back of the car and opened the boot. To his dismay, Lepski also got out of the car and joined him.

"Which is the luggage of the American gentleman?" the guard asked.

"These two blue bags."

"Please tell him to bring them to the customs' house."

Duvine turned to Lepski.

"They want to check your bags."

"What the hell for?" Lepski took out his police warrant and shoved it under the guard's nose. "Tell him who I am!"

Feeling a trickle of sweat run down his face, Duvine said, "This gentleman is a highly placed American police officer. He doesn't want his bags disturbed."

The guard examined Lepski's police warrant and shield. From his expression, it made no impression on him.

"The gentleman doesn't speak French or German?"

"No. He is American."

"What's he say?" Lepski demanded, and began to shuffle his feet as his temper rose.

The guard eyed him with interest. Lepski's habitual war dance before his temper exploded was something new to the guard.

"The gentleman needs the toilet?" he asked Duvine.

"What's he say?" Lepski demanded in his cop voice.

"He's asking if you want to take a pee," Duvine whispered. "He is puzzled by the way you are jumping up and down."

With an effort Lepski controlled himself. He made a noise like an electric drill biting into a knot of wood. The guard took a step back and gaped at Lepski.

138

"Lepski! Stop making an exhibition of yourself!" Carroll exclaimed, sliding out of the car and joining them. "Do what the man says!"

The guard turned to Duvine.

"Please tell the gentleman that we have instructions to check all luggage owned by Americans. We regret the inconvience, but those are our instructions."

"I understand," Duvine said, his shirt sticking to his back with cold sweat. "Do you need to search my baggage?"

"That will not be necessary."

"What's he say?" Lepski demanded.

Duvine explained.

"It won't take long, Tom. Just go along with them."

"Do it!" Carroll snapped. "Why must you always make a nuisance of yourself?"

Lepski clenched his fists, choked back an expletive, then said in a strangled voice, "Okay, okay, so let this jerk go through our goddamn bags! Why should I care?"

Duvine lifted out the two blue suitcases belonging to the Lepskis.

"Just these two?" the guard asked.

"The rest is mine," Duvine said. He handed the cases to Lepski. "Take them in, Tom. It won't take long."

The guard handed Lepski back his police warrant, then leading the way, he conducted Lepski, carrying the two suitcases, to the customs house.

"He's forgotten my vanity case!" Carroll cried.

Duvine very nearly slapped her.

"Forget it!" he whispered urgently. "Your perfume could cause trouble."

"If you say so." Carroll got back into the car. "Oh, I do wish Tom wasn't so difficult!"

"He has so much character," Claudette said, forcing a bright smile. "These Swiss! I do wish he hadn't all this bother."

"He really loves it," Carroll said. "Don't worry, honey, about him. It'll be something he will bore his friends with when he gets home."

Duvine joined Lepski in the customs house. He found him

shaking hands with the Head official who spoke English.

This man, introducing himself as Hans Ulrich, was profuse with apologies.

"Mr Lepski," he was saying, "it is this Russian icon affair. All our frontier posts have been instructed to search the luggage of all American visitors. My man was only doing his duty. Of course there is no need to check your baggage. I can't remember when we ever had an American police officer pass through our frontier. Let me tell you it is a great privilege." He turned to the guard. "Take Mr Lepski's bags back to the car."

Duvine closed his eyes and drew in a deep breath of relief.

Leaving Lepski, now beaming, to talk to Ulrich, he followed the guard, took the two suitcases from him and put them in the boot, slamming the lid.

"What is happening?" Carroll demanded.

"Tom's getting the VIP treatment. No problems," Duvine said as he slid under the driving wheel.

He and Claudette exchanged quick glances.

The last hurdle had been crossed. The icon had arrived in Switzerland.

Now for Lu Bradey. Now for the switch. Then Radnitz.

eight

During breakfast, served in their room, Lu Bradey explained to Maggie what he wanted her to do. He sat in a chair while Maggie, lying in bed, munched a crisp roll, smothered with black cherry jam.

"I am expecting people to arrive sometime this morning," Bradey said. "I don't know exactly when, but it will be in the morning. I have business with them. I don't want you to be around while I'm with them. I want to talk to them in this room. Are you following me, baby?"

Maggie reached for another roll and began to butter it.

"You want me out of the way? Right?"

"Yeah. First, I want you to pack. Then I want you to take all the things out of your vanity box. I want the box empty. Are you still with me?"

Maggie spread a layer of black cherry jam on her roll, her pretty face slightly contorted with concentration.

"What shall I do with the things from my box?"

Bradey sighed.

"Put them in one of your bags."

Maggie nodded, her face relaxing. She began to munch again.

"I love this jam!" she exclaimed, her mouth full. "I know I shouldn't be eating this bread. I'll be getting fat!"

Bradey sighed again.

"Enjoy yourself, baby, and listen."

"I'm right with you, pet. I empty the box, pack all my things and . . . what else?"

"Once you have packed, you take the elevator down to the basement, go through the tunnel to the swimming pool."

"But I will have packed my swimsuit, or won't I have?"

Bradey ran his fingers through his hair.

"Forget your swim suit. You won't be swimming. You will sit by the pool in the sun and wait until I join you. Got it?"

"I just sit and wait?"

"I'll get you a book. There's a new Harold Robbins just out. You dig his books, don't you?"

Maggie's face brightened.

"I adore them! The sexy bits turn me on."

"Okay. So you sit by the pool and read, and I'll join you as soon as I can. Right?"

Maggie finished her roll, poured more coffee, then nodded.

"If that's what you want, honey."

Bradey sighed with relief.

"Fine. After my business talk, we'll leave. Now, Maggie, it is very important I should find you at the pool. I haven't the time to look for you if you wander away. As soon as my business talk is over, I want to leave. Understand?"

"I just sit by the pool and read Harold Robbins?"

"That's what you do. Now, if you have finished breakfast, please pack."

Maggie examined the breakfast tray, was surprised there were no more rolls, sighed and got reluctantly out of bed.

The time now was 09.15.

"While you are packing, baby, I'm going down to settle the check. Don't forget to empty the vanity box."

Leaving her, Bradey took the elevator down to the reception lobby.

Sergas Holtz was sitting in the lounge where he had a

142

clear view of the reception desk. Sure that the Hall porter would be puzzled as to why he was always sitting in the lounge, never going out, Holtz had taken the precaution to explain to both the Hall porter and the reception clerk that he was expecting an important telephone call and had to wait until it came. This explanation satisfied the curiosity of the hotel staff.

He watched Lu Bradey pay the bill. He wandered over to the reception desk and began to study one of the travel folders while he listened.

"I will be leaving shortly," Bradey was saying to the reception clerk. "Mr Willis will be arriving around two o'clock. Send someone up for my luggage in half an hour."

"Certainly, sir."

Bradey then left the hotel and hurried to a bookshop just up the street and bought a copy of the new Robbins novel. Then returning to the hotel, he entered his room. He found Maggie, having had a shower, leisurely dressing.

"Get moving, chick!" he said, a snap in his voice. "They'll be up in half an hour for the luggage."

This statement immediately threw Maggie into a panic. She began to stuff anything she could lay hands on into her suitcases.

"Not the goddamn bath towels!" Bradey shouted. "Oh, for God's sake! Get dressed! I'll do it!"

By the time the porter came tapping on the door, Bradey had emptied the vanity box, packed the suitcases and put the vanity box out of sight. By this time, flustered, Maggie was dressed. He told the porter to put the bags in his car.

"Now, baby," he said firmly, "here's your book. Go to the swimming pool and wait. Right?"

Maggie nodded.

"You will really come for me, honey? We really are going to get married?"

"Just wait," Bradey said, his patience nearly exhausted. "I'll come for you and we'll get married."

When she had gone, after kissing him, Bradey wrote a note, put it in an envelope and addressed it to Mr Pierre Duvine. He took the note down to the reception clerk.

143

"Please give this to Mr Duvine when he arrives."

"Certainly, sir."

Still watched by Sergas Holtz, Bradey returned to his room, took a chair out on to the balcony where he could watch arrivals and sat down to wait.

Two maids came into his room. He told them to go ahead, explaining he was waiting for friends. They stripped the bed and did the bathroom for the afternoon arrival of Mr John Willis.

At 11.15, Bradey saw the Duvines and the Lepskis arrive. He came in from the balcony, lit a cigarette and began to pace up and down. The note he had left with the reception clerk told Duvine Bradey's room number and urged him to come to him at once.

Sergas Holtz watched the Duvines and the Lepskis book in. He watched the luggage porter put four suitcases and a blue vanity box on his trolley and wheel it away. He watched the Duvines and the Lepskis with the reception clerk enter the elevator. He nodded to himself. Very soon now, his long boring wait would be over, and there would be action.

At their doors, Duvine said, "Suppose we all meet in the lobby in half an hour, Tom? We'll take a look at the town."

"Fine with us," Lepski said. "This is some hotel. What's the food like?"

"You won't starve," Duvine said, and steered Claudette into their room and closed the door. "Bradey's here. He wants to see me at once. His room's right by ours."

"Be careful, my treasure," Claudette said, a little anxiously. "Lu is very tricky."

Duvine kissed her.

"Then so am I. I'll be right back."

Bradey paused in his pacing as a tap came on his door. He went to the door and opened it.

"Pierre!" he exclaimed. "Marvellous to see you!" and he grabbed Duvine's hand and pulled him into the room. "You're looking terrific!"

Not to be out-done, Duvine pumped Bradey's hand and exclaimed, "You don't look a day older! My God! It's good to see you again."

Both these two were expert con-men. They appeared to exude friendship and genuine pleasure to see each other again.

"Tell me," Bradey said, still holding Duvine's hand. "Don't keep me in suspense. Any problems?"

"None, except the Lepskis are driving us crazy."

"The customs?"

"Went like a dream."

Bradey beamed.

"I knew I could rely on you. Now the switch."

"Yes." Duvine made a little grimace. "That will need handling, but I can do it. Have you the duplicate box?"

"Of course." Bradey produced the vanity box. "It's empty, Pierre. It won't take you more than a few minutes to transfer Mrs Lepski's junk, then come to the Eden hotel, Zurich, where I will be waiting with twenty thousand beautiful Swiss francs for you."

Duvine rubbed his hands.

"Marvellous!"

"How will you get rid of the Lepskis?"

"I will tell them my mother is ill and we have to return to Paris. Leave that to me. God! Won't we be glad to see the last of them!"

"Right. I must get off." Bradey gave Duvine his wide, false smile. "You have done a swell job. I'm going to insist Ed pays you another ten thousand."

"Why, thanks, Lu! That's terrific!"

The two men shook hands.

"See you in Zurich . . . maybe two days?"

"The moment I've done the switch, I will be with you. It depends on the Lepskis. They cling to me like glue. Yes, two days, could be three. I'll call you at the Eden."

"Perfect. Good luck, Pierre," and with more hand shaking, more friendly smiles, Bradey hurried to the elevator to find Maggie.

Duvine picked up the vanity box, looked to see if the corridor was deserted, then quickly went to his room.

When Claudette saw the vanity box, her face lit up.

"All right, my treasure?"

145

"No problems. He's even promised to give us another ten thousand." Duvine gave a happy laugh. "He hasn't the faintest idea that we are going to double-cross him. Imagine! A miserable thirty thousand Swiss francs when we can get at least four million dollars!"

Claudette threw herself into his arms, and they began to waltz around the room.

Bradey found Maggie sitting in a sun-lounging chair engrossed in the Robbins novel.

"Come on, chick," he said. "We're on our way."

Maggie was lost to the world, her eyes popping as she read on. Bradey snatched the book from her.

"Come on!"

She blinked up at him.

"Oh, Lu, do let me finish what's happening. He has her on this bed . . ."

"Never mind! We're on our way!"

He bustled her across the road and to where his car was waiting.

As he drove towards Villeneuve, he once again went over the instructions how to get to the Zurich autoroute, the name of the hotel, and for her to wait for him.

She parted with him a little tearfully when they arrived at Villeneuve, but she was now so happy with her new watch and the money he had given her and the thought of finishing the Robbins novel, she controlled her emotion. She finally drove away to the autoroute to Zurich after Bradey had assured her a dozen times he would join her in not more than a week.

Bradey had already arranged to hire a Golf VW from a local garage. He walked to collect it, then drove to a commune swimming pool and rented a cabin. The pool was fairly full of young people on a late vacation. None of them paid him any attention. He took his suitcase into the cabin, locked the door and set about transforming himself into a wizened, smartly dressed old man who could have been a retired banker or an attorney. It wasn't until 01.30 that he returned to the Montreux Palace hotel and booked in as Mr John Willis.

146

Sergas Holtz who was still sitting in the lounge would have been completely fooled, so brilliant was Bradey's disguise, had Bradey not made the error of using the same suitcase as he had used when booking in under the name of Lewis Schultz. Holtz, trained to observe, recognised the suitcase as the porter carried it to the elevator, followed by Bradey. Holtz remembered his uncle had warned him that Lu Bradey was a master of disguise. Holtz gave a satisfied little nod. Any time now would be the time for action. He had seen the Duvines and the Lepskis leave the hotel. He went into the bar for a quick snack.

Up in his room, Bradey unpacked his bag. He took out a Smith & Wesson .38 pistol.

Following Ed Haddon's instructions, he had stopped at Geneva and had driven to the address Haddon had given him.

A tall, fat man in his early thirties, and apparently covered with coarse black hair which grew from his face like a wasps' nest and sprouted out of his shirt collar, was happy to sell him a gun as soon as Bradey mentioned Haddon's name.

Bradey loathed firearms. He loathed any form of violence. He stressed that the gun must be unloaded and watched the tall, fat man empty out the cylinders. Satisfied the gun was non-lethal, Bradey put it in his pocket and paid.

Now, he sat on the bed and examined the gun uneasily. He hoped he wouldn't have to threaten Duvine. If he did, he didn't think he would be very convincing. Duvine had seemed so friendly. It was hard to believe he was thinking of double crossing him. Haddon was suspicious of everyone, but Bradey decided he must take no chances with Duvine. A million dollars was a million dollars. He then thought of Maggie. Maybe it had been a little rash to have promised to marry her. Bradey sighed. He couldn't see himself settling down with Maggie for years. She was the type who would lose her bloom of youth early. Well, there was time. He first had to get the icon. He put the gun back in his suitcase, then feeling hungry, he went down to lunch.

Lepski didn't approve of Montreux. He admitted the view across the lake and the steamers were pretty good, but the town itself seemed as dead as George Washington. Carroll too was a little disappointed, but she loved the watch shops and kept lingering to stare while Lepski made impatient whistling noises.

The Duvines were nearly at the end of their patience. They kept exchanging looks, encouraging each other that this ordeal couldn't last much longer.

"How about eats?" Lepski said. "What are the steaks like?"

"Never eat a steak here," Duvine said hurriedly. "They are not in your class. Let's go to a pizzeria. It'll be a change for you." He had now made up his mind not to offer the Lepskis any further sophisticated food, and although he knew he was libelling the Swiss to say their steaks weren't up to standard, he just couldn't stand watching Lepski saw through yet another steak, grumbling. To his surprise both Carroll and Lepski liked the big pizza set before them.

"Now this is what I call a meal!" Lepski said, beaming. "Like home."

Knowing that Claudette had already sown the seed for the Lepskis to visit Gstaad, Duvine, while they ate, brought his mother on to the scene.

"I'm frankly worried," he said. "She wasn't too good when we left Paris. I called when we were in Monaco and heard the old lady has taken to her bed."

"Gee! I'm sorry," Lepski said, looking concerned. "I lost my old lady four years ago, and I still miss her."

Duvine lifted his shoulders.

"It may be all right. I'm calling tonight, but if she isn't better, Claudette and I feel we should go back."

"You should," Carroll said. "I'm terribly sorry."

Duvine smiled.

"I may have better news. Anyway, if we do have to go back, it doesn't mean you have to. You must see Gstaad. You'll love it."

"You two have been marvellous to us!" Carroll exclaimed. "If you have to go back, why shouldn't we all go back? I think Paris is more fun than Switzerland."

Somehow Duvine kept a smile on his face.

"You say that because you don't know Gstaad. Now that's really a place! Liz Taylor has a villa there, and she wouldn't live there unless it was real fun. You want night life? It's there, strip tease: gorgeous girls: dozens of night clubs. Steaks? Let me tell you, the genuine Kobe steaks are flown in every day from Japan: thick and juicy: the best steaks in the world! Then there are gorgeous mountains, snow, rides in horse-drawn sledges, and the shops! You've never seen shops like they have at Gstaad!"

Claudette who had been to Gstaad and had thought it a dreary hole, hoped God would forgive her husband for such outrageous lies, but she realized it was essential now to get rid of the Lepskis.

Lepski listened, his eyes brightening.

"Strip tease? Gorgeous girls? Juicy steaks?"

"Ask yourself why Liz Taylor would live there if it wasn't the in-thing."

"Sounds terrific!"

"I would be very, very unhappy to think you two, coming so far, should miss Gstaad." Duvine looked imploringly at Claudette.

"They just must go," she said firmly. "It's an experience of a lifetime."

"Okay, then we'll go," Lepski said, "but we'll miss you two."

"We'll miss you too," Duvine lied, and signalled for the bill. "This may not happen. I hope to get good news of my mother tonight. I long to see Gstaad again myself. Now, I'll drive you to Vevey to see the famous swans." He smiled at Carroll. "You can take some marvellous photographs. Then this evening, we'll take a steamer. There's music and dancing and we can dine on board. You'll just love it!"

So they went to Vevey and Carroll, intrigued by the swans, used up two rolls of film while Lepski contained his impatience. He thought if you've seen one goddamn swan you've seen the lot. A bunch of rather dirty-looking swans didn't impress him.

Then they returned to the Montreux Palace hotel, agreeing to meet in the bar at 20.00, and then go to the boat station. None of them noticed an elderly, wizened man sitting in the lounge who watched them as they entered the elevator.

*   *   *

In their room, Duvine turned to Claudette.

"I can't stand it any longer!" he exclaimed. "Those two are driving me out of my mind! I am going after the vanity box tonight! Now, sugar, we meet them in the bar and I'll tell them I have had a telegram from my brother about my mother's condition. He will be calling me at nine thirty, so I must stay here for the call. You will take the Lepskis on the steamer. You'll be back around eleven o'clock. I will be in the lounge and will tell them we must leave at once as my mother is sinking. We'll pack right now. As soon as you have gone with them, I'll switch the boxes and put our luggage and the Lepskis' box in the Mercedes. I'll tell Lepski it will be quicker for us to drive back to Paris as there's fog at Geneva. I will tell them to ask the Hall porter to get them a Hertz car to take them to Gstaad."

Claudette considered this.

"You don't think they'll want to come with us?"

"Not after the build-up I've given Gstaad. Did you see the look in Tom's eyes when I mentioned steaks from Kobe and gorgeous girls?"

Claudette stifled a giggle.

"What a shock for him when he gets there!"

"To make certain, I will tell him I've booked them into the Gstaad Palace hotel: the best."

"But, my treasure, the Palace doesn't open until December."

"He won't find that out until they arrive. Come on, sugar, let's pack."

At 20.00, the Duvines entered the bar, both looking worried. The Lepskis were already there, and Lepski was wrapping himself around a double Scotch while Carroll was getting acquainted with a double dry martini.

Seeing the Duvines' expressions, Lepski asked, "Trouble?"

"I hope not." Duvine sat down, after pulling out a chair for Claudette. "I've had a telegram from my brother. He says

150

mother is pretty bad, and he will telephone me tonight to tell me if I should return or not."

"What a shame!" Carroll exclaimed. "I'm so sorry."

"Yeah. That goes for me too," Lepski said. He signalled to the barman. "Maybe it won't be all that bad. What'll you have?"

"Scotch for me and a martini for Claudette, please," Duvine said. "As you say, it may be all right." He waited until their drinks were served. "Although I have to stay here, Tom, you three must go on the steamer trip. When you return, I could have good news."

"Oh, no!" Carroll exclaimed. "We can't go off and leave you to sit and worry. Oh, no!"

"She's right," Lepski said. "Let's sit right here and wait. We can eat at the hotel."

For a moment, Duvine was non-plussed, then his fertile con-mind sprang into action.

"There's no need for that, Tom, but I appreciate your consideration. You're both real friends, but do me a favour. Claudette has never been on a steamer at night. She has been so looking forward to it." He didn't look at Claudette who only kept her expression of surprise controlled with an effort. "Will you take the girls, Tom? Carroll will love it too. There's no point in all of us missing a trip like this. Please be nice and give Claudette some pleasure."

Put like that, Lepski couldn't refuse.

"Why, sure. You leave it to me. I'll give the girls a ball."

Having experienced an evening on a Swiss steamer at night with an accordion and a violin producing sounds only the Swiss love, elderly, fat people prancing, and pork chops for dinner, Duvine doubted they would have a ball. He relied on Claudette to make a pretence of enjoying herself.

"Thank you," he said, and looked at his watch. "The steamer leaves at nine o'clock, so maybe you'd better think about getting ready to leave."

Hastily finishing his drink, Lepski got to his feet.

"Okay, girls," he said. "Let's go."

The elderly, wizened-looking man who had been reading

151

a newspaper while nursing a Scotch on the rocks, watched the party leave the bar. Then he got to his feet and wandered into the reception lobby as Lepski led Carroll and Claudette to the revolving doors.

Duvine also watched them, then he walked to the elevator. The elderly wizened-looking man entered the elevator with him and walked away down the long corridor, followed by Duvine.

In his room, Duvine waited a few minutes, then cautiously opened his door and looked along the long, deserted corridor.

Lu Bradey had his door ajar and remained waiting with a clear view of the Lepskis' door. He didn't have to wait long. He watched Duvine, carrying the vanity box he had given him, move silently to the Lepskis' room, pause for a brief moment as he manipulated the lock, open the door and enter the room, closing the door behind him.

Uneasily, Bradey fingered the Smith & Wesson gun in his jacket pocket. He waited. Minutes ticked by. He knew Duvine would have to transfer Carroll's things from one box to the other. He knew Duvine was a quick, expert worker, but the wait made Bradey sweat.

Then he heard voices and saw a young couple leaving their room. They were obviously very much in love. As they walked towards his room, he stepped back, closing the door, then reopened it as they paused outside the Lepskis' room to kiss. At that moment, Duvine, carrying Carroll's vanity box, moved out into the corridor.

The young couple broke apart, giggled and hurried down the corridor.

Duvine paused to relock the Lepskis' door, then walked fast to his room as Bradey stepped into the corridor.

"Sir!" Bradey exclaimed. "Excuse me."

Duvine paused and looked at this elderly, wizened-looking man. He frowned.

"Yes?"

Bradey walked towards him.

"A moment, sir."

"I'm sorry. I am in a hurry."

By this time, Bradey had reached Duvine.

"That was very nicely done, Pierre," he said. "I knew I could rely on you."

Duvine felt a rush of hot blood to his head. He stepped back into his room, followed closely by Bradey.

"You?" Duvine managed to say. "Lu?"

"Of course." Bradey forced a laugh. "I've changed my mind, Pierre. I am taking the box to Zurich." He closed the door. "There is no point in you driving to Zurich. Ed wants it this way."

Still holding the vanity box, Duvine was so shaken he sat down abruptly.

"I've talked to Ed," Bradey went on. "He's agreed you have done a swell job. I can pay thirty thousand Swiss francs. I have the money with me."

Duvine's sharp mind began to function. His immediate reaction was to knock Bradey unconscious and bolt, but he couldn't leave without Claudette who wouldn't be returning for another two hours. No, he told himself, this situation called for diplomacy.

"That's a marvellous disguise," he said. "Sit down for a moment. Let's talk."

Bradey hesitated, then sat down, away from Duvine.

"What's there to talk about, Pierre? I want to leave for Zurich tonight. Ed's expecting me."

"I know what's in here," Duvine said, tapping the vanity box. "The Catherine the Great icon."

Bradey nodded. He slipped his sweaty hand into his jacket pocket and fingered the gun. It didn't give him any confidence.

"The icon is worth at least ten million dollars," Duvine said, watching Bradey closely.

"It might be if a buyer could be found," Bradey said cautiously.

"Ed wouldn't have organized the steal unless he had found a buyer. I know who the buyer is . . . Herman Radnitz."

Bradey shifted uneasily. So Haddon had been right. This scene was set for a double-cross. He looked at Duvine's powerful build. One punch from him, Bradey thought, sweat on his forehead, could be lethal.

"You are jumping to conclusions, Pierre. Anyway, what's in the box is no affair of yours. You were hired to steal the box and you've done a great job. You are being paid generously. There is nothing more to discuss. Give me the box and I'll give you thirty thousand Swiss francs."

Duvine shook his head. He could see Bradey was scared and he flexed his powerful muscles.

"There is something to discuss, Lu. Let's be realistic."

"I'm not following you." Bradey forced a quavering smile. "You and I have worked marvellously together for years. I can still put a lot of profitable work your way. What do you mean . . . realistic?"

"Come on, Lu!" Duvine put on a ferocious scowl that made Bradey edge back in his chair. "Here's my proposition: we drop Haddon out of this deal, and we split the take between us. We pick up three, even four, million each. What do you say?"

"What do I say?" Bradey's voice shot up a note. "I say I don't believe this is you talking, Pierre. I am surprised and shocked. I don't double-cross my friends. Ed is my friend. I thought you were my friend. Give me the box, and I will give you the money, and we will forget this conversation."

Duvine eyed him, then shook his head.

"No. You either accept my deal or you don't get a thing and I take the lot. I am in contact with Radnitz. He'll buy from me. He doesn't regard you nor anyone as a friend. There's nothing you can do about it, Lu. Will you come in with me or be a loser?"

Haddon had foreseen this double-cross, Bradey thought. Haddon always foresaw trouble and was always prepared for it.

He shook his head.

"You haven't thought this through, Pierre. Radnitz wouldn't deal with you. He won't even deal with *me*. I will deal with his agent, and you don't know who his agent is. Now let's stop this nonsense. Another thing: Haddon could make your future life a misery. I give you my word I won't tell him about this. Give me the box, I'll give you the money, and we go on together as we have always done."

Duvine hesitated, then thought of what it would be like to own five million dollars. He also thought of Claudette who had so much faith in him.

"No! You've had your chance. I keep the box, and there's nothing you can do about it!"

Bradey sat still for a long moment, fingering the gun in his pocket. He was now desperate. If he threatened Duvine with the unloaded gun, would Duvine launch himself at him and do him an injury?

Gathering his courage together, he said, "But there is," and produced the gun which he pointed at Duvine. "I'm sorry, Pierre, but you have asked for it."

Duvine stared at the gun, feeling a cold rush of blood down his spine. He, like Bradey, had a horror of violence. Never before had anyone pointed a gun at him, and the sight of the small black menace in Bradey's hand turned him into a white-faced, trembling travesty of his usual confident self.

"You . . . you wouldn't dare shoot!" he gasped.

Bradey, startled that here was a man even more cowardly than himself, had a rush of bravado. He leaned forward, waving the gun at Duvine and snarled, "I wouldn't kill you, but I would cripple you! I'll blow off your knee cap if you don't give me that box at once!"

Duvine shuddered. With a trembling hand, he put the box on the floor and shoved it with his foot to Bradey.

"Don't keep pointing that gun at me," he quavered. "It . . . it might go off."

Bradey snatched up the box, stood up and backed to the door.

"You are a fool, Pierre. You won't get any more work from us, and don't forget, Ed never forgives a double-cross."

He opened the door, stepped into the corridor and made quickly to his room.

Ten minutes later, he was speeding towards Zurich, Carroll's vanity box on the passenger's seat by his side.

La Suisse, brilliantly lit, steamed towards the Montreux boat station. From it exuded the wailing of a violin and an accordion.

Pierre Duvine watched it approach. He had been waiting for the past hour, and by now, he had recovered to some extent from the crushing blow Bradey had dealt him. He still felt utterly depressed. Not only would there be no millions, but no money from Bradey. He was in a fever of anxiety. He realised he had no further future in antique swindles. He knew Haddon would pass the word, and no one would touch him. His shop in Deauville without new, stolen goods would have to close. The red light had gone up when he had lost at the roulette table. His luck had run out! He had gambled on getting at least three million dollars and he had lost. He had just enough Swiss francs to buy gas for the journey back to Paris, and back there, he knew the rent demand would be waiting and other bills. Well, he told himself, back to picking pockets. The Paris season was about to begin. The city would be full of rich tourists, flashing their wallets. He hated the risk, but he had to face up to the fact it was the only way to keep off the bread line. He thought of Claudette. She was his only consolation. She would accept, without complaining, the inevitable. She would understand he couldn't have done anything when faced with a gun. He felt a surge of love for her run through him. How blessed he was to have Claudette!

La Suisse came alongside the jetty and people began coming down the gang plank. Duvine could see Claudette and the Lepskis, and he waved.

Lepski was thankful to get off the steamer. To him the night trip had been the biggest drag he had experienced. The sounds made by the violin and the accordion had set his nerves jangling. The fat, elderly couples who danced happily made him make noises like a flat car battery trying to start an engine. The pork chop dinner had made his jaws ache. Carroll, seeing how Claudette was apparently thrilled with everything, controlled Lepski as best she could, but she too was thankful to get off the steamer.

Claudette, her face set in a smile, had wondered how Pierre had been succeeding. She felt a complete wreck after forcing gaiety for so long, trying to make the Lepskis happy and praying such an experience would never happen to her again.

One look at Duvine's white, strained face told her there had been a disaster.

"Pierre?" She ran to him.

"We must leave at once!" Duvine said. "She's dying." He turned to the Lepskis. "I'm sorry. I know you will understand. We must drive to Paris. Geneva airport is closed through fog. We mustn't waste a moment." He caught hold of Lepski's hand and wrung it. "Dear friend, please don't delay us and please excuse us. We should have been on the road an hour ago, I have arranged your room at the Palace, Gstaad. The Hall porter will fix you with a car and tell you how to get there." He turned to Carroll. "We'll write as soon as we get to Paris. So sorry about this. It's been wonderful meeting you both."

As Lepski and Carroll tried to convey their sympathy, Duvine signalled to Claudette to get in the car. She gave them a mournful wave of her hand as Duvine slid under the steering wheel.

Dazed by the suddenness of this, the Lepskis could only wave as the car shot away. As Duvine headed for the autoroute, he told Claudette what had happened.

"I don't know what we'll do!" he said in despair. "We are nearly out of money. To think that devil Bradey should have a gun!"

Claudette patted his hand.

"Nothing matters, my treasure, so long as we have each other," she said.

They were the most comforting words Duvine had ever heard.

Lepski stared after the tail lights of the departing car, then turned to look at Carroll.

"Well, for God's sake! That was quick, wasn't it?"

"The poor dear is losing his mother, Tom," Carroll said a little tearfully. "What do you expect?"

"Yeah, I guess that's right. We'll miss them." Lepski started across the road to the hotel entrance. "What an evening! That music! That meal! I thought I would blow my lid!" '

"You're always grumbling!" Carroll snapped. "This is the Swiss way of life. You should be grateful to see how other people enjoy themselves."

Lepski made a noise like a tractor back-firing. An elderly couple passing, stopped and stared at him.

"Lepski!" Carroll snapped. "You're making an exhibition of yourself!"

Lepski glared at the elderly couple and then stamped into the hotel lobby.

"You had better arrange about a car for tomorrow," Carroll said.

Lepski grunted and walked over to the Hall porter's desk.

"I want to rent a car for tomorrow morning," he said. "My friends have had an emergency and have gone off in the car we were sharing. Bad about the airport shutdown."

The Hall porter lifted his eyebrows.

"Geneva airport is open, sir. There's no fog."

Lepski's cop mind became alert.

"That a fact?"

"Certainly, sir. What kind of car would you want to rent?"

"Wait a minute," Lepski said. "We are planning to drive to Gstaad. We are booked in at the Palace hotel."

"The Palace hotel isn't open yet, sir. The Gstaad season only begins on December 1st."

Lepski loosened his tie: always a sign that he was getting heated.

"Tell me, friend," he said. "I understand Gstaad is noted for their Kobe steaks. Right?"

"Well, no sir. You mean the Japanese steaks featured so much in Hong Kong? They are not imported to Switzerland."

Lepski dragged at his tie.

"I understand there are strip tease shows with lots of gorgeous girls."

"Perhaps in the season. Around Christmas, sir."

Carroll joined Lepski.

"I don't think we will be going to Gstaad," Lepski said through his teeth.

"What do you mean?" Carroll demanded impatiently.

"Quiet!" Lepski snapped. "I smell trouble!" He went over to the reception desk. "We'll be leaving tomorrow," he said. "Have my check ready please."

"Mr Lepski? Room 245?"

"Yeah."

The clerk produced a detailed statement.

"That, of course, sir," he said with a bright smile, "includes Mr and Mrs Duvine's check. Mr Duvine was in a hurry. He told me his mother was dying. He said you would take care of the check." He looked inquiringly at Lepski whose face had turned wooden.

"Yeah," Lepski said. "I'll take a look at this," then taking the statement, he walked back to Carroll, "I want a drink."

"Can't you think . . . ?"

"Quiet!" Lepski snapped, and Carroll, seeing the danger signs, followed him into the bar that was almost deserted. Lepski sat down and began to study the items on the statement. He looked at the final amount and released a low, long whistle.

The barman came over.

"A treble Scotch on the rocks," Lepski said. "You want something?" This to Carroll.

"No! You drink too much! What's the matter? Must you look like someone out of a horror movie?"

Lepski said nothing. He waited for the drink, swallowed half of it, then looked at Carroll.

"The old rum-dum Bessinger was right. She warned us about dangerous people. I said all along that Duvine was a con-man; but you wouldn't listen."

"Don't start that all over again! What are you talking about?"

"We've been taken," Lepski said. "I'm ready to bet my last dollar that that sonofabitch hasn't ever had a mother!"

"Lepski! What are you saying?"

"It's the oldest con trick in the world! We've fallen for it! We're landed with their hotel check, his drinks, food and a couple of items he bought in the hotel for his charming bitch of a wife," Lepski snarled. "And what is more . . ." He

159

went on to explain that the season at Gstaad hadn't begun: no hotel, no Kobe steaks, no gorgeous girls, no nothing.

"I can't believe it!" Carroll cried, then seeing the expression on Lepski's face as he glared at the hotel check, she realized what he was saying had to be true, she flew into a rage.

"We must tell the police!" she hissed. "No one takes us for a ride! No one!"

"We'll do nothing of the kind," Lepski said quietly and firmly. "If it ever gets out that an American police officer had been taken for a ride by a smooth, goddamn con-man, I'd never live it down! The boys back home would laugh themselves out of their fat minds! I warned you, but you wouldn't listen. It's your money." He dropped the statement into her lap. "Let this be an experience, and from now on, don't trust anyone!"

Carroll looked at the amount she would have to pay and gave a little scream that made the barman look sharply at her.

"Oh, Tom!"

"My old man said you have to pay for experience," Lepski said. "In the future, listen to what I say."

Carroll nodded.

"Now, I'll ask you something," Lepski went on. "Have you really enjoyed your trip?"

Carroll hesitated.

"Well, it has been a bit disappointing, but this just makes a mess of it, doesn't it?"

"Yeah. Tomorrow we'll go home. I've had enough of Europe. We would have been smart to have put all that wasted money in the bank. Is there anything left?"

Carroll grimaced.

"Less than five thousand."

Lepski patted her.

"That'll take care of our debts." He finished his drink, then stiffened. "Jesus! I've forgotten our neighbours! Now, listen, you must tell them, as I'll tell the boys, we have had a marvellous time. Not a word about the goddamn food. You remember those fancy meals we had to eat? Okay, you make

160

your pals green with envy. Tell them about that duck we had. Ram it down their throats. Show them those photographs you took of the swans, the mountains, the Eiffel tower. No one . . . repeat no one . . . must have an idea we haven't had a ball. Right?"

Carroll brightened. She could imagine how she would keep her girl friends enthralled and goggle-eyed. Maybe, being the centre of attraction for the next few months, would be worth the trip.

She got to her feet, linked her arm in Lepski's and gave him her best sexy smile.

"Let's go to bed, Tom."

Knowing that smile, Lepski couldn't get her to the elevator fast enough.

Lu Bradey parked his car outside the Eden hotel, Zurich, took the blue vanity box and his overnight case and entered the hotel.

The time was 01.15.

The night porter received him.

"Just overnight," Bradey said. "I believe you have a Mr Claude Kendrick here."

"Yes, sir. He is waiting for you in the bar."

"Just take my bag up to my room. No, I'll keep this box. It's a present for Mr Kendrick's daughter."

Carrying the box, Bradey walked into the bar. He felt triumphant. In spite of Duvine, and thanks to Ed Haddon, he had accomplished his task. In a couple of days he would be worth a million dollars.

He found Kendrick sitting in an empty bar, a bottle of champagne in an ice bucket on a table beside him. Kendrick looked up expectantly, but seeing this elderly, wizened-looking man, grimaced, but then he saw the blue vanity box and he jumped to his feet.

"Lu, my dear boy! What a disguise! It is Lu?"

Bradey gave a joyous laugh.

"Yes, it's me." He waved the vanity box. "Success!"

"My dear, dear darling!" Kendrick exclaimed. "I knew you could do it! How wonderful!"

"When I'm asked to do a job, I do it." Bradey put the box on the table, poured champagne into Kendrick's glass and drank. "But there was some trouble."

"Bad?"

"Never mind. I handled it. Duvine tried a double-cross."

"How dreadful!"

"I fixed him. This is the last job he gets from us. Let's go upstairs, Claude, and open the box. When will you get the money?"

"Tomorrow. I have an appointment with Radnitz. I told him you would be arriving. He said he would have the money ready."

"Marvellous! Let's go to your room."

As the two men walked to the elevator, Kendrick said, "I have brought the necessary tools to open the box. We must be very careful not to damage the icon."

"You'd better let me do it," Bradey said. "I've got the know-how."

Up in Kendrick's room, the door closed and locked, Kendrick gave Bradey a set of tools, then sat down to watch.

While he worked, Bradey gave Kendrick a running commentary of how he had outwitted Duvine. Kendrick, listening, made little gasping noises.

"Who would believe it?" he said as Bradey levered the sides of the box apart. "Do be careful, chéri. It would be a dreadful thing to even scratch such a precious object."

"Here it is," Bradey said and gently lifted out a slab of wood from the false bottom of the box. "All these lovely millions."

Then both men stiffened and stared at the slab of pine wood. Kendrick, his heart missing a beat, snatched the slab of wood out of Bradey's hands.

"This isn't the icon! It's just a piece of wood!" he said huskily.

The shock was almost too much for Bradey. He snatched the slab of wood out of Kendrick's hands, glared at it, then threw it on the floor.

Duvine had outwitted him! Somehow he had managed to switch the boxes, but how? As soon as that sonofabitch had stolen the Lepskis' box, he hadn't been out of Bradey's sight.

Kendrick suddenly rose to his feet.

"You double crosser!" he screamed. "Give me the icon. I . . ."

"Shut up!" Bradey snarled. "It's Duvine! He's probably with Radnitz right now, offering it at half price!"

Kendrick closed his eyes. He knew Radnitz wouldn't hesitate to deal with Duvine. He thought of the money he had spent, setting up this steal. He thought of Louis de Marney waiting for his share. He knew there was nothing he could do, but return to his Gallery.

He waved feebly to the door.

"Go away. Don't ever let me see your horrid face again," he said, then taking out his handkerchief, he burst into tears.

The previous evening, Sergas Holtz walked into Herman Radnitz's study and placed a blue vanity box on the desk.

"Your instructions, sir, have been carried out," he said.

Radnitz smiled.

"Excellent! Tell me about it."

Holtz looked bored.

"There was no problem, sir. The Lepskis with their friends went out to lunch. Bradey went to the restaurant also for lunch. I took the opportunity and switched the boxes."

"Have the box opened and let me see the icon," Radnitz said.

Holtz took the box and left the study. He handed the box to Mythen.

"There is an object concealed in the bottom of this box," he said. "Mr Radnitz wants to see it," and he walked away.

Half an hour later, Mythen entered Radnitz's study, and with reverent care, laid the Catherine the Great icon on the desk before Radnitz.

"A magnificent treasure, sir, if I may be permitted to say so," he said.

Radnitz picked up the icon, his toad-like face alight with pleasure.

"You are right, Mythen," he said. "One of the greatest treasures in the world. See if you can contact Vasili Vrenschov. Tell him to come as soon as he can."

It wasn't until the following day, when Pierre and Claudette Duvine were planning to get rid of the Lepskis, and Bradey was disguising himself as John Willis, that Vrenschov's Beetle VW drew up outside Radnitz's villa. He plodded up the marble steps with the heavy tread of an old man.

Mythen opened the front door, looked sharply at Vrenschov and asked, "You look poorly, Mr Vrenschov. You are not well?"

"No. I will not be staying for lunch," Vrenschov said, his fat face the picture of gloom.

"Not staying to lunch? That is most unfortunate. The chef has cooked a special pheasant pie for you. Are you sure?"

Vrenschov moaned softly.

"I will not be staying to lunch."

"That is most regrettable, sir. Please follow me."

Radnitz had seen the shabby VW arrive. He had placed the icon on his desk. He sat back, clasping his fat hands and completely relaxed. Either way he couldn't lose, he told himself. If the Soviet government wouldn't give him the Dam contract, at least he would get eight million dollars for the return of the icon, but of course to get the Dam contract was much more important.

When Vrenschov plodded into the study, Radnitz knew immediately the Dam contract wasn't to be his. Well, all right, he had the icon. Not the ace card, but at least the king.

"Come in, Vasili," he said, a rasp in his voice. "What is the news?"

"Unfortunately, Mr Radnitz, my people have decided to postpone the building of the dam for several years. They accept your estimate, but due to the sudden economic crisis, due to the shortage of grain, they feel money should not be spent on the dam."

"But perhaps after this crisis?" Radnitz asked, his toad-like smile stiffening.

"We can but hope."

"At least, they accepted my estimate?"

Vrenschov nodded.

Radnitz pointed to the icon.

"You see, Vasili, I have got this precious work of art. What do your masters say? Are they prepared to pay me eight million dollars for the return of this magnificent treasure?"

Vrenschov looked like a man about to die.

"I fear not, Mr. Radnitz."

Radnitz stiffened. He glared at Vrenschov.

"What are you saying? This icon is one of the oldest possessions Russia owns! It is worth twenty or even more million dollars! It has caused the President of the United States to be embarrassed. What will they give me for it?"

Vrenschov crushed his greasy hat between his hands.

"I fear nothing, Mr Radnitz."

Radnitz reared back.

"*Nothing?*"

"I have talked to the Minister of Arts," Vrenschov said. "He is a great admirer of yours, Mr Radnitz. He has instructed me to confide in you a state secret in view of the fact that you are such a good friend of our country. Thirty years ago, when Premier Stalin was our ruler, the Catherine the Great icon was stolen. No one knows who stole it. The then Minister of Arts knew he would be placed before a firing squad if the news leaked out. He had a very clever replica made and this replica has been on show at the Hermitage until it was stolen from Washington." He pointed a trembling finger at the icon on Radnitz's desk. "That, sir, is the replica. The Minister of Arts told me to ask you to accept it as a souvenir of your continued interest in the Soviet Union."

He turned and practically ran out of the room, leaving Radnitz staring bleakly at the icon.

THE END

》》 If you've enjoyed this book and would like to discover more great vintage crime and thriller titles, as well as the most exciting crime and thriller authors writing today, visit: 》》

The Murder Room
Where Criminal Minds Meet

themurderroom.com